IN DOG WE TRUST

In Dog We Trust

edited by

Anthony Cowin

BLACK
SHUCK
BOOKS

Black Shuck Books
www.BlackShuckBooks.co.uk

First published in Great Britain in 2018 by
Black Shuck Books
Kent, UK

Edited by Anthony Cowin
Original concept and story selection by Anthony Cowin and
Matthew Cash.

978-1-913038-28-1

ACKNOWLEDGEMENTS

Thanks to Matthew Cash, Theresa Derwin and Phil Sloman for all your help in bringing this book together. A huge thank you to Steve Shaw for his unfaltering patience and support. Thank you also to Jilly Rivers and all the wonderful staff at Birmingham Dogs Home for all their wonderful work in caring for and rehousing those wonderful dogs.

Finally thank you to those people from around the world who responded to the social media appeal that sent in clippings from their local newspapers relating to the horrific recorded in this book. These historic records will one day help the survivors and their children to understand what happened in that dreadful time the media now call The Year of the Dogs.

Anthony Cowin, 2018

FOREWORD

Emma Green

I write this watched over by my housemate's Border Collie, who is currently resting his chin on my knee and doing his very best to be cuter than my screen. He's a being that I sometimes suspect may be entirely too smart for his own good. Without sheep to tend to, he distracts himself by guarding his sovereign domain, the stairs, and admits safe passage only to those who can trade in the best of belly-rubs. If he ever realises that world domination would be a fine way to alleviate his ennui... then God save us all. We needn't work hard to imagine this wild scenario, however, since this anthology has already done the work for us in a series of short stories that ask: what *would* happen if man's best friend became better than man?

As humorous as the idea might sound, it offers fertile ground for thought-provoking narratives. One of the greatest gifts of storytelling is that it offers us the chance to step out of our lives and into others, and what better life to inhabit than that of a dog? For while humans have shared our homes and livelihoods with the humble hound for around 20,000 years, science is only just beginning to fully plumb the depths of how radically different their world is to ours.

Quite what this world is like is hard to say but we know for starters that it is one defined by their noses, seeing that their sense of smell is somewhere between

10,000 – 100,000 times more accurate than the average human's. This means that their awareness of odours far outreaches ours, not just in terms of distance but also in time. A dog, quite literally, can smell yesterday. If this isn't sign enough of their dominance, consider that they can hear in frequencies twice as high as a human. Shoring up your anthropocentric pride with the old folktale about dogs only seeing in black and white won't work either because the evidence suggests that dogs can see all the colours available to human vision other than the red-green spectrum.

All this means that our canine friends possess superpowers that we can only dream of, such as the ability to hear sounds a quarter of a mile away or smell pregnancy and cancer. They are also furry Little Brothers that can sniff out if you've recently had sex, broken your promise not to smoke, exercised or not, and what you ate last night. Dogs, quite literally, know truths that we have little, or no, access to as humans.

In these ways, dogs inhabit that uncanny territory, so fertile for storytelling, in which the familiar becomes as strange as any alien planet. By fictionally entering their perspective we not only glimpse other ways of living but fresh ways of seeing and understanding our own reality.

By considering how civilization would arise around such different senses and bodies our eyes can be opened (or, in dog terms, nostrils widened) to just how contingent human civilisations and mores really are. We are also introduced to a whole range of entirely original possibilities for drama. Dog Romeo would have smelt the drug on Juliet's breath, leaving the pair to chase cars into the sunset together. Elizabeth Bennett would have understood her admirer's affections sooner had she only been able to sniff Dog Darcy's butt. Dog Jane Eyre wouldn't have been trapped in 'the red room', just 'the room' but would have probably still whined and scratched at the door to be let out.

In his excellent novel *Solaris*, Stanislaw Lem wrote that – "We have no need of other worlds. We need mirrors. We don't know what to do with other worlds. A single world, our own, suffices us". There is much to be unpacked from this quote but most interestingly, to my mind, is what I understand as an acknowledgement that it is an oversight of speculative fictions to think that our mirrors need always be green, tentacled and capable of piloting their way through wormholes. Our very best mirrors may ultimately be those that have lived under our noses all along, one of which is currently resting its own nose on my knee in the hope that I'll share my lunch. To read about the perspectives of dogs is, in short, to develop our appreciation of what it is to be human.

Emma Green, 2017

Birmingham Dogs Home

Birmingham Dogs Home – helping homeless dogs find happier tomorrows for over 125 years, with a mission to rescue, reunite, and rehome the lost and abandoned dogs from around the West Midlands and South Staffordshire. With no Government funding, public support is a vital lifeline to this Charity. More information can be found at www.birminghamdogshome.org.uk, or by calling 0121 643 5211.

Registered Charity Number: 222436
Company Registration Number: 662947

The Wild Life of Jenny Friars

By AMY WARD

Big Brother starlet hot favourite to host new wildlife documentary series.

She may not have emerged from the house as winner earlier this year, but Jenny Friars has perhaps proven to be the most bankable star of the lot, and certainly the most surprising.

The lads mags may love her, but Friars is rumoured to have turned down a recent lucrative modelling offer to focus on a "serious" television career. And she's off to a promising start.

Park Life comes from the same team responsible for the acclaimed Outback and Rainforest and will focus on national parks around the world, this time with a face in front of the camera. Jenny Friars, 25, has admitted to being approached for the role. "It's an exciting opportunity. Not only will Park Life show us the wonders of the world, but it will reveal something of our place in it, too."

Park Life is due to hit our screens next year.

Painted Wolves

Ray Cluley

I've seen things few other people in the world have ever seen. And it's a pretty big world, you know. The term 'small world' is a bullshit expression used to explain coincidence, if you believe in that sort of thing. I know you don't, Jenny. "Everything happens for a reason," you said once. As if it's part of some plan. But whose? I don't know. I believe in Darwin. If there's a God, and if He has a plan, then He not only works in mysterious ways but cruel ones too. I've travelled a lot of the world in this business, and it's a bloody big world, and it's beautiful, absolutely beautiful, but it's fucking brutal. We're all part of that.

When the sun came up today I was thinking about how lucky I was to see the things I see. We were looking down at those zebra. You were drinking from a bottle of water. Tony and Eddie were prepping their cameras. The sky was lightening into shades of red and you said, "red sky at night", which didn't make much sense at the time because it was morning. Later you told me the rest of it: red sky at night, shepherd's delight, red sky in the morning, shepherd's warning. You didn't know what it meant though. Anyway, I was watching the sun rise, and I was glad to see it, and I was watching you, and I was glad for that as well, and all around us Africa woke up. The rising sun brought the volume up with it, wildlife waking in a rich medley of calls and caterwauls. You didn't have to be a sound technician to appreciate it.

"Beautiful," you said.

Eddie clapped –"Okay, let's go,"– and we took our positions. You put one foot on a rock, hands on your knee, and watched the sun fatten into a fuller shape, all for the camera. I remember wondering how many of our future viewers would watch the sunrise and how many would focus on the way your shorts clung to the curves you made in that pose. You knew I was looking. You knew we all were.

"Africa," you said, turning to face the camera. "Still very much a wild continent, even in Kruger National Park. Perhaps especially in the park. Here, over a thousand different species exist together in a purposeful circle of—"

"Perpetual."

"Perpetual. Fuck."

Tony swore, too. I let the furry shape of the microphone dip into shot while I rested my arms (you take every opportunity) and you apologised to Eddie.

"Go again."

Your face was red in the glow of the rising sun. "Africa. Still very much a wild continent..."

This time you messed up the name of the park.

"Fuck, fuck, fuck!"

"Gee, do we need to have the sun coming up as she says it?" Tony asked.

"There's always tomorrow," I offered.

"No," said Eddie. "There isn't. We lost too much time with the lions. Come on, go again."

The sun was almost up, drifting away from the horizon to add a bloody colour to the soil of—"Africa..."

"Fucking cunt!"

Tony peered into one of his cameras. Some dirt had gotten in despite his precautions. I remember you covering your ears, claiming, "Ladies present," though we'd all seen your *Big Brother* footage and knew better.

"Fucking Africa!" Tony yelled. Fucking Africa got its own back, though, and Tony jerked his head down with a squint and another, "Fuck," rubbing wind-blown dirt from his eyes.

You laughed, I remember that, too. Tony glared. You covered your mouth with both hands.

The others didn't like you much. You have to remember, the three of us had worked together for a while, sharing tents and toilet paper in some right God-awful places. Then you came along. "Time to put a pretty face in front of the camera," they told us. "No more voiceover." Admittedly, your celebrity status, such as it was, gave us something of an Anti-Attenborough advantage. Tony and Eddie both admitted that much, at least, even if they did call you 'the tits with the script'. One of the magazines said of *Park Life*, "I'm sure there will be lots of interesting animals, but most eyes will be on the beautiful creature that is Jenny Friars." You pretended to hate it, said it was sexist and patronising, but you didn't mean it. It would get you more work and us more viewers, and you understood that. All we had to do was film the damn thing.

"Calm down, mate," Eddie said. He was squatting at

the stove with a sandwich on a stick, making jaffles. Real food, apparently. Just Eddie being the typical Australian, I suppose, only happy when burning food over an open flame. He was a canyoneer with legs like a rugby player and muscled everywhere else from years of carrying heavy gear. He was spooning something from a can to his mouth even as he cooked.

"I hate this country," Tony told him.

"You hate every country we film in."

"Yeah, well, every country makes it difficult for me." He puffed breath at the lens and tilted it to catch the light.

Tony and I had worked together on a series called *Rainforest* and after that we'd done *Outback*. With *Rainforest* we picked up a dose of dengue fever and botfly. With *Outback* we picked up Eddie.

"You okay, Tom?"

You asked me that a lot. When you looked up, you smiled. I'd been staring at your midriff as you tied a knot into the front of your shirt. I suppose you must have noticed. I tried to smile back but you had a way of making it feel crooked, like I'd forgotten how.

"Hot enough?" you asked.

A more confident man would have turned that into some sort of flattering joke, but me, I just laughed and wiped the sweat from my brow. My shirt would be soaked before breakfast. You, though, you wore yours with a sort of serenity. Even khaki looked good on you.

"Hey, Tom," Eddie called, "chuck me my bag, mate."

Do you remember asking me why I let him push me

around? It was the 'mate'. Every time Eddie said 'mate', it didn't feel so bad. "He's okay," I'd told you, "once you get to know him."

"You just mean he's a dick but I'll get used to it."

I'd laughed. You knew a bit about people and how to put up with them, I suppose. Seemed that way, on *Big Brother* I mean, but that might just have been the way it was presented. That's the thing with TV stuff. It's all about the editing.

Tennyson once wrote that nature was "red in tooth and claw", and it's true. I've seen it. In Africa alone I've seen a baby giraffe pulled to pieces by a pack of hyenas, a wildebeest split apart in a crocodile tug of war, and an elephant brought down by a pack of hungry lions. I know it's supposed to be a pride of lions but when you're sitting in the middle of it, 'pack' feels far more appropriate. Pride suggests a nobility that just isn't there. It's hard to see a lion as the king of beasts when his mane is matted with blood where he can't lick it clean. If he's a king, he's a savage one.

Following that group of zebra, we were actually hoping for some of that tooth and claw. We'd filmed them interacting, of course, their feeding habits, social activity, but really we were waiting for something else. They're beautiful creatures, zebra. Serene. Born to be on the screen, it seems, but doomed to be prey. That's what we were waiting for.

And that was what we got.

You were the first to notice it happening. "They've seen something," you said. "Or maybe they've heard something."

You were right.

Eddie pointed. "Look."

"Beautiful," said Tony.

In the grass, rising from the dusty ground, was a motley mix of colour. Orange, red, brown, and black, all of it blending together in dirty patches. Spots of colour like rusty stains.

"And there. Look."

"How many's that? Ten? Twelve?"

African hunting dogs. Wild dogs. *Lycaon pictus*, or 'painted wolf'. A formidable group of them, too. They're small, but what they lack in strength they more than make up for in numbers.

By the time we had the cameras on them they were trotting towards the herd of zebras at a steady six, maybe seven, miles per hour.

"They're picking up the pace," I said.

The herd saw them and fled.

"Look, look, there they go!" You checked to see which of the cameras was on you and turned back to face the action. I had the boom pole overhead, ready for whatever you might say.

"They've singled one out."

The African hunting dog is a pack hunter. With agile prey like gazelles or impala, they have to be, flankers cutting off escape routes and narrowing the choices of their prey. With the zebra, though, it's a straight chase.

"Look at them go!"

The pack focused their attention on one of the young females. When the first of the dogs leapt, you startled me with a sharp gasp. The dog tore into the zebra as it landed, dragging its claws across the animal's hide as it slid back down over the rump. The zebra kicked it away with a rear hoof, but the dog re-joined the chase as a new lead attacked, leaping to grab hold of the zebra's muzzle. It sank its teeth into the soft sensitive flesh of the zebra's mouth and clawed at the face. With its head forced down, the zebra slowed enough that the other dogs could attack its hind legs, clawing at the muscle, piling onto its back. They tumbled together in a cloud of dust and a high cry of pain from the zebra. There was a mad scrabbling as the zebra tried to stand, dogs tearing at its flesh, but it was too late. It had been too late from the moment it hit the ground. One of the dogs got hold of an ear, more by accident than design, and tore it free. Worse than this, though, the soft flesh of the zebra's underbelly was exposed. We watched as the animal was disembowelled alive, the pack clawing out its insides as the poor beast kicked for all it had left. One of the dogs burrowed its way into the stomach. Two others yanked at the legs, making a wide V of them until eventually one was torn free from the body. And still the zebra struggled, writhing and rolling as best it could beneath a mass of dirt-furred bodies. I was relieved when one of them finally clutched the zebra's throat closed in its mouth and yanked the animal dead.

We actually celebrated, do you remember? Eddie,

Tony, you, me: we all gave muted congratulations, hissed a quiet "yes!" of success and high-fived like we'd played a part in the spectacle ourselves. I guess we had, in a way: we'd watched and done nothing. Nothing but film it, anyway. But the African hunting dog, the wild dog, is one of the world's most efficient and elusive predators and we had caught the entire thing on film. It was amazing, something to put us with the heavy hitters. Shit, even *Planet Earth* hadn't caught a wild dog kill on camera. It was just luck, really. Ours, not the zebra's. We'd been in the right place at the right time, that was all. It would've happened whether we'd been there to see it or not.

Although we'd been quiet with our congratulations, something aroused the attention of the dogs. Maybe the wind changed. They looked over at us, a dozen or so all at once. It was eerie that shared reaction. They didn't run, not with a fresh kill, but they watched us as we watched them. One of them held the zebra's severed tail limp in its mouth. It was a great shot.

Nature, red in tooth and claw. Caught on film.

"But the African hunting dog is also a very social animal…"

My words, your voice, right to the camera as we filmed follow-up footage. With some animals the violence didn't necessarily end after the main event – there could be fighting over the carcass – but the dogs, they shared their spoils equally. Even a latecomer who had missed the hunt was provided for.

The remaining zebra stood grazing, not very far away at all. They could probably see what the dogs were doing if they looked but they kept their heads down, safe for the time being as the dogs ate and played and napped.

"Let's do that again without the but," Eddie said, covering other editing choices; the kill may have been the first thing we filmed but it wouldn't necessarily be the first thing you saw by the time it hit the screen.

"Why, what's wrong with my butt?"

You turned your back to the camera and bumped your behind left and right, shimmying it down in a provocative wiggle. This was the Jenny we knew from *Big Brother*. A little bit of Z-list celebrity, shining through, wanting to be a star.

"Fuck's sake, Jenny."

Tony had only been filming for a few minutes, but he was already getting irritable. A few minutes feels a lot longer when you're lugging camera equipment around under an African sun. I was feeling the same strain. I had the sound mixer in my shoulder satchel, cans clamped over my ears, and the boom pole raised so that the armpits of my shirt were exposed for all to see just how much I was feeling the heat.

You did that thing where you wipe a hand down over your face, straightening your expression into something more serious. 'Emotional reset' you called it. Or Davina did. Someone.

"The African hunting dog is a very social animal..."

Occasionally, as you spoke, one of the dogs would raise its head from where it dozed with the pack or look back from where it stood panting in the dry air. Did you feel them watching? I did. I can still feel them, even now. All the way down here. Their breath is hot on my skin.

It happens to everyone at some point, I'm told. This connection between man and animal. A friend of mine once saw an elephant brought down by lions in the dead of night. He watched the whole thing unfold in green-tinged light on a night monitor and it stayed with him forever after. Elephants bleat, did you know that? My friend used to hear that sound in the dark whenever he tried to sleep, an elephant's bleating struggle as a tawny carpet of lions writhed on its body. Someone else I'd known a few years ago saw a Komodo dragon bite a buffalo then stalk it for days until the poison claimed it. You're not supposed to interfere in this job. You just let it happen and record it, impartial, as nature runs its course. But it gets to you sometimes. I mean, how natural is it to watch something suffer and do nothing?

Not that there's anything I could have done. Not about the dogs. Not about any of it.

"...prowling for prey in highly organised units, or simply relaxing together, howling in play."

I liked the rhyme of that. It chimed well. Prowling and howling. Prey and play.

"Good," said Eddie. "Now the other way around."

You turned your back to the camera again –"Like this?"– and began reciting the same lines. I don't know if you were joking or not but Tony made no attempt to hide his frustration either way. "Christ, Jenny, stop pissing about."

The narration felt clunky second time.

"Okay, cut there," said Eddie.

I brought my arms down with relief and you stepped away from the descending microphone, exaggerating your dodge and ducking dramatically with a cry of, "Watch it!"

The dogs skittered. They didn't move far, but they were suddenly alert and looking our way.

Nobody said anything. Your smile disappeared without needing an emotional re-set.

We waited.

Slowly, one by one, the dogs began to leave. They took as much of what was left of the carcass as they could carry.

"Shit."

"Film me," you said, motioning us all at you with beckoning hands, "film me, film me."

"Jenny—"

But Eddie had his camera up and so Tony followed suit. Eddie said, "The dogs," and Tony turned to film them walking away.

"The pack moves in single file, the alpha male leading, but for much of the day they will sleep the heat away in the shade..."

And so on, as you improvised a way for us to edit the footage together. Eddie encouraged you with quick hand-rolling gestures and I tried to think some script your way. You even shifted your position, squatting down in the dirt so the shot could look like a separate occasion, gesturing behind as if the dogs were still sitting somewhere nearby. It was good.

"In Kruger National Park, there is a predator easily identified by the blotchy colours of its coat. Shades of orange, brown, and black, with a long tail tipped in white, this is the 'painted wolf', better known as the African hunting dog…"

I kept glancing at them. The heat rising from the ground turned them into wavy shapes, phantoms, and before long they were gone altogether.

"You okay, Tom? Want some water?"

You tried to pass me your own bottle but I had little chance to take it, grabbing wildly at the side of the truck instead as we bounced high and came down hard. We always sat in the back with the equipment, you and me, because we were the smallest. Even as cramped as it was we spent a lot of our travel time up in the air and then slamming our behinds. We got banged around a lot making sure the equipment didn't.

"Woah! That was a good one. Here."

I took the water, more because you'd offered than because I was thirsty.

"Do you think we got enough back there?"

You were worried you'd screwed up.

"We got enough," I said. "We'll probably only use three minutes or so."

"Really?"

"Yeah. Probably just the kill, and a little bit of what

came after. Lucky we were running behind schedule or we might have missed it."

You smiled, and said, "Everything happens for a reason."

"Yeah. I suppose it does."

Eddie slowed the truck. I looked around in case he'd spotted something and I thought maybe – "What's going on?" You had to shout to Eddie over the sound of the engine.

"Dogs," I said.

But after a quick look you shook your head.

I couldn't see them either. The sky was taking on a darker hue. The sun was going down, a trick of its light and heat making one end seem squashed as it slipped below the horizon. Shadows were growing long and dark around us.

"Looking for a camp spot," Eddie yelled back.

"But the caves are so close. We might as well keep going."

"Not in the dark."

"You've driven at night before."

"Yeah, but it's rockier now, and I don't really want to be fixing a tyre again, not out here. Not at night."

We were already on our last very-patched spare, and the early hours of evening increased the risk of puncture, maybe worse, thanks to the poor visibility.

"But it's okay to camp here at night?"

You had a good point. "I'm sleeping in the truck," I said.

"I'm done with sleeping in the fucking truck," Eddie said.

And of course, Tony supported that. "Nothing to be scared of here," he said, "There's nothing but us."

"Well, I think I'll join Tom in the truck." You smiled. "If that's okay with you?"

As if it wouldn't be.

In the early days of the shoot, sleeping had been difficult. Do you remember? We'd been following those lions, sleeping whenever they did, which often meant during the day, which always meant we were hot and sweating and attracting flies and not actually sleeping much at all. In the open bed of the truck there wasn't much protection against the incessant buzzing of flies or their frequent landings. Not much protection against lions, either, for that matter, though they turned out to be rather dull. Placid. Did you ever play that game, sleeping lions? We used to play it at school. You had to lay down and pretend to sleep while someone else played hunter, moving among the sleeping lions and trying to get them to move. You weren't supposed to touch them but you could get close and whisper, say things to make them stir. Of course, we couldn't do that, not with real lions. We took turns napping at night, but following lions over the rise and fall of Africa made that nearly impossible and even when we were able to stop driving for a while the lions growled constantly. A low, throaty sound. Engines in muscled flesh. All of it made everybody tired and irritable. A bit tense, as well.

It was like that the night after the dogs, too. Unpacking the truck, setting up camp, I could feel a building growl, and little irritations flitted around like flies.

"If only we had a heli-gimble," Tony said, looking back the way we'd come. Thinking of the dogs, probably.

"If only you'd stop saying that."

That got you the middle finger without him so much as glancing around. From me, a smile, but I doubt you noticed.

"If only we had a helicopter to mount the heli-gimble on, eh?"

That was the best I could do.

Tony was right though; it would have been a great bit of kit to have. Three sixty degree filming, good long shots, good close-ups from even a kilometre away… But bloody expensive, and we were still low budget. None of this 'three years in the making' with us. No slow motion predator action or time-lapse prey decay.

I was setting up a light in the back of the truck, along with a monitor and one of the cameras we did have. I wanted to check the infrared for when we were in the caves. I wanted to distract myself.

"You all right, Tom?"

"Hmm? Yeah, I'm fine. Just, you know…" I held up a memory card, titled and dated, adding the details to the index in my notebook. If I didn't do it, nobody would.

Eddie glanced at us. "He's not fine," he said. "That kill got to him. What's wrong, mate? Tooth and claw and all that shit, remember?"

That annoyed me. Partly because he was right, it had bothered me, but also because until that moment the distraction had been working just fine.

"You're either spots or stripes in this world. Dog or a zebra. Sad, but true."

"I'm fine," I said again. "Looking forward to the caves."

That was a lie, but I thought it would change the subject because Eddie was looking forward to them. A seasoned canyoneer, much of his campfire talk had been of his hikes and climbs in the Australian Blue Mountains. Sorry, the 'Blueys'. Not really mountains but a plateau eroded into mountainous shape. Anyway, it worked, although he quickly turned the conversation around to one of his 'Nam stories, climbing around the caves of the Annamite Mountains. He'd also explored some of the Hang Son Doong in Phong Nha-Ke Bang which was supposed to be our next stop after Africa. The Hang Son Doong, or 'mountain river cave', is the biggest cave passage ever measured. The Echo Caves, though, are some of the oldest caves in the world. They haven't been fully measured yet, and we had special permission to explore further than any of the offered tours.

"You really staying in the truck?" Tony asked. I was spreading my sleeping bag out on the floor near the monitors. I shrugged.

You tossed your bag to me as well.

"Let us warn you about Tom, love," Eddie said, but that was all I heard. I looked up to see him making a tiny hook with his little finger. Tony laughed.

"Never had any complaints," I said.

You gave me your most dazzling smile yet, said, "Tom, you sly dog," and I remember thinking *this is what I need to be like? This is how I get you to notice me?*

"Friend of mine did this cave a few years back," Eddie told us. "For *Planet Earth*, I think. Gomantong. You guys see it?"

I knew the episode and nodded with Tony.

"Yeah," Eddie said. "Gomantong." He smiled at me. "That was full of shit, too."

Tony roared with laughter.

"No offence, mate," Eddie said.

I ignored Eddie to look at you. You gave us all a sort of half-smile. "I don't get it."

"Gomantong cave," Eddie explained. "It's—"

"A shithole."

Stealing his pun was the best I could do for retaliation. He scowled at me but recovered quickly.

"Yeah. It's a shithole. A cave literally full of shit. Guano. Friend of mine, Scud, good fella, he said that pile of bat crap was a hundred metres high and swarming with all sorts of things. Cockroaches, centipedes, crabs. All sorts of creatures. They never even had to leave the cave. That steaming pile had its own fucking – what do you call it? – ecosystem."

"You ever get crabs from a dirty hole, Eddie?"

I don't think you were sticking up for me. You were trying to get involved in the conversation. The new girl still trying to fit in. We'd talked about it before and you'd compared it to that *Big Brother* house, how it took the group a while to accept anyone new. It's the same with animals, although with animals it can be even more brutal.

Tony and Eddie barely acknowledged your joke before

discussing between them the technical difficulties we'd face filming in Echo Caves. I was concerned about the sound quality but of course they were preoccupied with the visuals. One of them said a rope pulley and counterweights would do it, and the other wanted a crane shot, but either way it was going to be a hassle lugging all the equipment around. You sided with Eddie, and Tony said you didn't know what the fuck you were talking about, you were just the tits with the script and you even managed to fuck that up. "The script part, anyway."

I said something pathetic like, "Hey, guys, come on," but it worked. Enough to create an awkward silence for a while, at least.

Tony, surprisingly, was the one to finally break it.

"Anybody got a beer?"

It was a joke wearing thin – he'd asked every night so far – but this time it was funny again and I think it was sort of an apology. Maybe that's why you gave me up.

"Tom's got a bottle of something."

Were you still just trying to fit in? Or were you doing your bit to accept his apology? Maybe you were simply deflecting the attention away from yourself for a moment.

"Is that true, Tom? You been holding out on us?"

I'd bought a large bottle of mampoer but I was saving it for celebrating the end of the shoot. I busied myself checking the connection between camera and monitor, pretending not to hear the question. Infrared is invisible to most animals, including humans, but the camera picks it up. I was able to see everybody in the camp even with the lamps off. It was sound that would be a problem in the cave.

"What are you doing, mate?" Eddie asked.

"Giving the gear a test run before the caves."

So much for pretending to not hear him.

"He's filming us for the DVD extras," you joked, and everybody laughed. I went along with it, glad some more of the tension was lifting.

"Is Jenny right? About the beer, mate?"

How could I not give it to them?

"Mampoer," I said. At Eddie's puzzled frown I added, "Brandy. Sort of. To celebrate our last day in Africa." I added that as a final attempt to put them off.

"Brandy?"

I smiled, and nodded, thinking Eddie's mockery might mean he wouldn't ask for it. And he didn't, because Eddie never asks.

"Let's have it, then," he said. "This is pretty much the last day anyway."

Everything is green and black when you film at night. Your skin was green on the screen. Eddie and Tony, too, though their eyes, looking at you, were dark pools of shadow. Shark eyes. You were crouching, doing an impression of Attenborough as if he was stalking around the campsite; good enough so we knew who you were doing but bad enough that it was funny. I'm half convinced it's how you got this gig in the first place because you did the exact same thing in the *Big Brother* house for one of their challenges or something. Everybody was laughing.

"And capturing what has never been seen before, not even by us at the BBC, with all our budget and big names like me... an African wild dog hunt."

"Fuck yeah," said Tony, raising his cup.

And you, still Jenny-Attenborough, "Please, Tony. Watch your fucking language."

The camera loved you. I zoomed it in.

You seemed to sense what I was doing and struck a provocative pose. "Make sure you get my good side."

"Which side is that?" asked Tony.

"They're all good," said Eddie.

"Aww, thanks, Eddie mate," you said, exaggerating your vowels, switching to Australian, "Not bad for a sheila, eh?" You turned and posed and turned again. Catalogue poses. Magazine parodies. Eddie smiled with his mouth but not with his eyes, not on the black and green screen.

And then behind Eddie, stepping quietly out of the night, was an African hunting dog. I could see it, panting, just over his shoulder. Behind Tony there was another.

"Yeah, that's good. That's your good side," said Tony. You were on all fours and looking behind with wide-eyed feigned surprise.

One of the dogs, with its head down, made a single bark at the ground. It was how they called to the pack, drawing them to the echo.

"Don't," I said.

"What was that, mate?"

You were all looking at me now.

"The dogs are back," I said. "They followed us."

Eddie and Tony looked at each other. Eddie took another mouthful of brandy. "They're miles away."

"No," I said. "They're here."

You couldn't see because of the dark, and because of how the lamps had ruined your night vision. Didn't stop you looking around, though. "Where?"

They were gone.

I checked back and forth between the monitor and the darkness around us. "They were here. They looked... I don't know. They looked hungry."

Tony exaggerated a sigh. "You're not going to start quoting Tennyson again, are you?"

"You're still shook up from the kill," Eddie said, "that's all. There's nothing out there."

He was right. Or half right. I couldn't tell. I panned the camera around but found nothing.

"They must be hiding. Waiting. For the right moment."

"People love to anthropomorphise animals,' you said. "You know; project human characteristics onto them. Maybe that's what you're doing?"

'Anthropo-what?" Eddie said. "That's a big word, sweetheart."

You grinned. "Oh, I like them big. The bigger the better."

"Seriously," I said. "The dogs..."

But you waved that away, "Don't worry about them," and teased me with, "I'll take care of you."

"You can take care of all of us," said Tony.

For him, you turned an imaginary crank at your fist to raise your middle finger. "Fuck you, Tony."

He raised his cup. "That's the spirit."

You raised your cup as well, but aimed the smile at me. Were you trying to include me? Or were you just posing for the camera? "To nature," you said. "Red in tooth and claw."

"And a bitch to get on film," said Eddie, tipping his cup to you.

Your eyes were vast dark circles, like the empty cavities of a skull. Caves in your face. I looked away from them and searched again for the dogs. I couldn't see them, not even with the night monitor, but I felt them out there in the dark.

Waiting.

✖ ✖ ✖

I've seen things few other people in the world have ever seen. I've seen birds of paradise performing their complicated mating dances, flashing their feathers like capes in a fashion show of arousal. I've seen colourful lizards leaping like acrobats to feed on swarms of black fly, a bright rainbow devouring a buzzing cloud. I've seen the peaks of the Himalayas, Ayers Rock, Victoria Falls. I've seen lots of beautiful things.

I've seen you.

But I've also seen a crocodile roll its prey. Heard the thundering chaos of splashing and devouring. Seen komodo dragons wait patiently for the inevitable, heard them hiss at a buffalo already dying. I've seen a zebra, serene, brought down by dogs that tore at her flesh and burrowed into her body. Seen them shove their way inside and—

"You okay Tom? Where are you?"

You...

...you...

...you.

Now I can't see anything. The dark here is absolute. But I must be quiet. Sound travels far down in the Mpumalanga escarpment. Down in the Echo Caves.

They exist because of erosion, these caves. Limestone. It covers approximately ten percent of the Earth's surface. Rain shapes it. Rivers sculpt it. The water, slightly acidic and loaded with carbon dioxide from the soil, slowly eats away at the rock. But over time it builds, as well, depositing calcite to make stalactites and stalagmites. It breaks and it builds, it wears down and it hardens, and all of it is very natural.

"Tom?"

I'll not say a word.

In Deer Cave, Borneo, there are three million bats. Three million at least, all flapping around in the dark. They use echo-location to navigate, hearing to see. Some animals do away with eyes completely in the caves, that's how dark it is. The Texas cave salamander, for example, devolving so it has no eyes at all. It doesn't have to see a thing. I envy it.

Sometimes it's better not to see. There's a cave in New Zealand that has a ceiling of stars, cave constellations held in an underground night sky. These beautiful glowing lights attract insects, drawn in by what they see, but the stars are not stars. The bright lights come from the bodies of glow worms that drop delicate strands of silk to trap their prey, hauling it up like a fisherman's catch.

Safer, sometimes, not to see.

"Tom? It's okay."

But just because you can't see something doesn't mean it isn't there. When oil in the Earth's crust releases hydrogen sulphide, a cave can be filled with dangerous toxic fumes. Poison you can't see. And when it mixes with the oxygen in water you get sulphuric acid, eating away at the world around it. That's how I used to imagine Hell. But Hell is a black and green screen that I'll carry with me forever. It's whimpering sounds, grunting sounds, growling away at my insides. Hell is the things I heard with my eyes closed. It's the sound of wild dogs with prey.

"Thomas!"

My name resounds in the dark and I hear an echo of it fade like the hiss of komodo dragons.

"You can come out now."

The 'now' echoes in the cave like a series of howls. They surround me. They keep me cowed, hunkered down in the dark.

I won't say a word.

�✗ ✗ ✗

"What do you like most out here?"

I wonder what would have happened if you hadn't asked that question. I wonder if, without that to think about, it would have been a normal night.

"The brandy," said Tony, upending the bottle.

"The wilderness," that's what Eddie said. "All this space and nobody around to watch everything you do. The freedom to do whatever you want."

"How about you, Tom?"

I shrugged. "You?"

You didn't hear it as an answer, but then you weren't meant to. You heard the question passed back.

"Same as Eddie, really," you said. "On *Big Brother* people watched everything I did, and most of it was stupid or embarrassing and really badly edited. They made me look like a bimbo. I like being a part of something serious now. None of that messing around in front of the camera."

"You've done that," Tony said.

"Exactly."

"I mean you've done that out here. Today."

"Hey, come on."

Eddie and Tony laughed.

"Seriously, they made me look like an idiot."

"I thought you looked pretty good," Eddie said.

Tony nodded. "The Jacuzzi," he muttered, but you heard him. You were meant to.

"That was part of a stupid game thing, and we were all drunk."

"We're all drunk," Eddie pointed out, though I don't think he was. Not at all.

"Yeah," said Tony, "So let's play a 'stupid game thing'." He span the empty mampoer bottle. A teenage game. A *Big Brother* game for no one to see but me.

I looked out into the darkness for the dogs. There was nothing at first. A turn of the camera, though, and I had them on the monitor. Two of them, maybe three, standing with their mouths open, panting despite the cool night air. Their eyes flashed from empty black to bright green when I moved the camera over them.

"We can't play that," you said, reaching to stop the bottle. "I'm the only girl."

"I know." Tony moved the bottle away and span it again. "This is just for deciding who's first."

You laughed. It sounded false to me, but to the others I don't think it made any difference.

You stood. "Right, that's it. Time for bed."

"See," said Eddie, "she gets it."

"Sorry, I've been fucked enough by a film crew already. Good night, boys."

On the screen the dogs were pacing. Agitated. There were lots of them now. Some of them growled. You looked around and I wondered if you'd heard them too but then, "Whoops," said Eddie as if you'd stumbled when really he'd pulled you down to the ground, into his lap. Maybe it was meant to be playful at first, I don't know, but then he gave you that crude grope – "Like that?" – and you clearly didn't; shoving him away should have been answer enough, never mind the way you spat his name. But like I said, Eddie never asked. Maybe he was telling you to like it. Maybe he just meant he did.

"Of course," Tony said, "It's only natural."

"Come on, Jenny, nobody'll know."

"No."

I heard you from over by the truck so they must have heard you, too. Even when the dogs started yipping and barking I heard you say no, and no, and I heard you say stop.

But Eddie didn't stop.

And afterwards, neither did Tony.

"Tom? We know you're in here."

I just want you all to leave me alone. So I push my way deeper, groping in the dark, forcing myself into narrow fissures of rock. It's wet, or cold, or both. I can't tell.

"We can wait, Tom. You'll have to come out eventually."

Troglodytes can go months without food. If I go deep enough, maybe I'll find something hungry enough to end this.

There are plenty of things in here with me. There's a baby giraffe. There's a wildebeest. There's an elephant, a buffalo, a zebra. You brought them with you, you must have done. Or maybe I did. They glow like stars that aren't stars, and they thrash and they mewl and they kick, fighting tooth and claw against something unseen. Maybe the darkness. I've seen these throes too many times. Heard them, too. Nature sounds wonderful when the sun's coming up, but it sounds very different in the dark.

"Tom."

Crouching in the darkness, hiding in caves we will never film, I hear the echoes of my name. It bounces my location back to you.

I imagine you surrounded by those others I've seen destroyed. I imagine you leading them, a procession into the dark to find me. A slow and ghostly stampede. I'll be mauled, gouged, rendered to chunks by tooth and nail and claw, crushed and broken by hooves and jaws. You're coming for me, and you're bringing all of them with you.

Teamwork. It's the key to successful mammal behaviour.

What I fear most, though, is that you'll find me and do nothing. That you'll just look at me. Record it in your memory and remain unsatisfied.

Something down here growls. It may have been me.

I can still hear the smacking sounds of flesh against flesh. I can hear the dogs, howling and barking and rutting in the dark.

It would have happened whether I'd been there or not.

There's nothing I could have done.

The things I've seen, the things I've heard. They wear me down, like water on limestone. And they harden me beyond calcite.

These caves are well named: I have become your echo: "No. No. Please. Don't."

Don't...

... don't...

...don't.

"Don't worry, Tom. Nobody will know."

No...

...no...

...no.

Rocks scatter under scrambling feet. Yours, mine, theirs. The animals.

"She's coming for me."

Laughter in the darkness. "I dunno about that."

Those sons of bitches.

"Did you film it, Tom?"

You know. You must know. I feel for the memory card in my pocket. Is that what you're after?

"Something for the DVD extras?"

Your words, but I'm no longer sure the voices down here have been yours. Maybe you're pretending to be someone you're not as well.

You're either spots or stripes in this world. Someone said that once. Was it you? Dogs or zebra. Predator or prey. But they get mixed up don't they? Plus tigers are striped, so that fucks up the analogy. It helps them hide. Helps them blend in.

But I'm no tiger. I'm a sleeping lion. You're just trying to get me to move and make a sound. You stir things up, that's what you do. Something you did, something you said, it stirred something up. In Eddie, in Tony. In all of us. Woke something. A sleeping dog best left lying.

I am Gomantong Cave. I'm full of shit.

"It's just nature, Tom."

"Come on, mate."

Come on. Mate.

I hear the dogs in here with me. They howl. And eventually, just as before...

I'll join in.

Student Asks For Help In Research.

By GOLDIE ANDREWS.

A local woman is asking for long-term residents to put on their thinking caps to help her solve a puzzle. Though student Kay has not specified what her project is about specifically she has included a photocopy of an old note she found in her home in the hopes of sparking memories from residents who may have been living in the area for the past 20-50 years. Is it a treasure hunt or is it just a university paper? Get in touch and find out.

MAN'S BEST FRIEND

Gary Fry

The council had promised to clean the house but there were dog hairs everywhere. Kay did what she could to vac the carpets around the little furniture she'd salvaged from her marriage...but never mind that; she had a new life to lead now. Despite leaving Sam after nine years, Kay had got through the first year of her degree and was enjoying her independence. She still cleaned rabidly, but this was now for her own benefit and not to keep the peace.

She'd lived most of her adult life in fear. Together since their mid-teens, she and Sam had remained too unsettled for children. He'd made a basic living from his window-cleaning round, and when she claimed loneliness at home he'd suggested a dog. He'd even sullied that, hitting poor puppy Molly almost as frequently as he had Kay. Yes, he'd taken the dog for regular long walks, but only because, as the rumours in the village had forewarned, he had other women to visit. When the university prospectus had dropped through the letterbox, Kay had decided at once. She'd apply to study animal psychology and then looked for rented accommodation near the campus. A year into her course, she'd been offered a council property and had made the bravest move of her twenty-five previously submissive years.

Molly was presently enduring the second mating

season of her seventh year and going wild. The dog still flinched from another's strong hand; Kay imagined she would herself, even though there was nobody around to administer one. This was difficult knowledge to accept; she kept forgetting, cowering with fright at the slightest sound. Perhaps she and Molly had been, as one of her lecturers had termed it, classically conditioned. It was dispiriting to think that they'd be this way forever. And so that autumn afternoon, the day after moving in, Kay became determined to overrule the past. She even spoke inspirational words to the dog. Molly recoiled immediately, making Kay realise that her goal wouldn't be easy to achieve.

They'd both loved Sam, in different ways. Kay understood why some women stayed with men who abused them: it wasn't always like that, there were periods of great romance; it was, in short, unpredictable – what was known in psychological literature as variable reinforcement. Indeed, the dog had enjoyed her frequent excursions across the village, each day probably a new house to explore. But Kay had found out better. The attention she'd received at weekends – takeaway, cuddles, Sam listening to what she might say – was always in advance of sex. Clearly, he hadn't screwed around when his lovers' husbands weren't at work. Kay had soon confronted him, which had led Sam to punish her disobedience before taking Molly out on the lead, perhaps the first time for genuine reasons. Her eye bleeding, she'd watched them side by side. It was a pity Molly couldn't make a realisation similar to her own.

Man's best friend, dogs were called, but that was only because they couldn't question their master's authority.

The new place wasn't perfect, just a back-to-back terrace with one bedroom and a flagged front yard. There was pleasant countryside nearby, however, and a dam at the foot of a slope, around which dogs could venture at will. Woods stood beyond, demarcated by a dry-stone wall bearing a single stile allowing access to walkers. Maybe now Kay could make use of the birdwatchers' binoculars Sam had once bought her, by way of an apology for another unwarranted assault. The old chap next door, with whom Kay had exchanged nods yesterday, was certainly an animal lover. She had no idea how many dogs he owned, but there were plenty. He let them roam on the grove, a quiet cul-de-sac that harboured few cars.

The man living in the house before Kay had apparently died in tragic circumstances. The council was legally obliged to reveal this, but only two other details: he'd taken his own life after his wife had left him but not inside the house. There was nothing else to remind Kay of this fact other than the black fur knotted in the threadbare carpets. The man had owned a dog, hardly surprising in this neighbourhood. Kay would surely get to know more about the case from the neighbours, though she wasn't sure that she wished to.

She'd done enough cleaning today. It was a good time to take Molly out for her walk; the September sky was darkening, a faint flittering pulse of rain occupying the atmosphere. If nobody was about in the fields, Kay might let the dog off the lead. She climbed into her jacket and exited to lock the door, before being dragged down the garden path at speed. Had Sam always maintained this pace, eager to reach his habitual destinations? Molly would have to learn to slow down – *if* she could; *if* irreversible damage hadn't already been done. There were other dogs on the grove and also on the grass verge leading her to the fence, the fields and the dam beyond. When she was out of the potential range of her next door neighbour – how many of these dogs were his? – Kay hissed to the animals, "Shoo! Go on, get away from us. I won't have my petal deflowered!"

She laughed at what her tutor had called "her propensity to use mixed metaphors", and it felt good. There'd been few opportunities to be cheerful since her childhood. It felt as if she were receiving as a gift something she'd always owned, but had foolishly mislaid, not a replacement but the original. The earth stretched before her like an absence of prison walls. Kay was so delighted that she stooped to set Molly free, too. The dog charged off into empty openness, kicking back grass in a savage parabola.

That was when Kay saw the man.

He was standing behind the wall in the indistinct shadow of the woods. The surface of the dam between the man and Kay glittered, casting up few reflections. She wondered why she'd sought the image of the man in the water; that made less sense than gazing his way, attempting to see who he might be. Not Sam, surely: he wouldn't have tracked her down. Nevertheless, the dark figure continued waiting at the stile, simply watching. But then Kay saw a black shape cross the gap in the stone and experienced instant relief.

He was only a guy out with his dog, after all. She summoned Molly (who'd been hastening for the dam) to the lead, reattaching her, just as she herself had felt. The dog baulked. Kay was annoyed with herself. Her resolve to escape the clutches of her husband had failed at a first hurdle, as if she'd suffered a conditioned reflex. She tramped up the hill, proverbial tail between her legs. The man at the stile merely shared her own predicament: a frisky dog to walk and space needed to do so. At the slope's brow, Kay turned before losing sight of most of the land. The man had now gone, though exactly where she couldn't figure out. There was no sign of his dog either.

Later that day – half a bottle of red dispatched with needful rapidity – she took Molly to bed with her. It was strange not having someone to cling to, however much the love she'd had for Sam had died. Kay arranged herself in the foetal position, drifting easily in and out of sleep, her dreams bad and then good but then bad again. At one stage, however, there was no such ambiguity: somebody was raging at her and she awoke with a start. But it was only Molly barking, her cries echoing in the unoccupied house. This wasn't the only disturbance, however. Could Kay also hear a scratching coming from downstairs? Was there whimpering, either plaintive or aggressive, woven into this sound, too?

Kay got up and strapped on a dressing gown. Molly continued protesting.

"Quiet, girl!" she admonished, mindful of the neighbours' opinion. Perhaps the dogged insistence at her front door – yes, as she exited the bedroom, Kay could now determine the source – was simply one of the old man's darlings, locked out overnight. Molly, scampering down the steps before Kay, finally reached the door. It was locked, but how wise would it be to open up at this hour? She was a woman alone in her nightwear. She hushed the dog (both animals now appeared to have fallen silent) and paced into her lounge. She reached the bay window from which she could see the whole front yard. Her heart pounding, she pawed back the curtain.

The yard was deserted. It was raining gently. The nearest streetlamp was two doors up, and it was in its limey light that the stage was set. *Crufts without a champion*, Kay forced herself to think, steadying her flesh, the rising hairs on the back of her neck. The blackened scrawny shape in front of the hedge across the grove must be an old conifer withering, and whatever skittered in the breeze beneath it, a clump of uncoupled foliage. Dew made the conifers glisten faintly. Kay shut out the night and retreated upstairs.

Before crawling back under the sheets, she opened the window. She would deal with any other disturbances more efficiently. Kay manoeuvred Molly into a position which felt mutually protective and then strove for more sleep; there was more work to do in the house the following day. Wakefulness faded, her misbehaving mind put down...but then it was suddenly resurrected. Somebody had stepped into the room, the floorboards creaking. No more here, thank you: she'd already checked the building and it was empty. The cold sensation at her cheek must be the window letting in air; there was certainly a sound of *breathing* nearby. That would be Molly, of course, but Kay couldn't now feel her. Had the dog dropped to the carpet, having grown too warm in bed? Only sheer obedience, or maybe also terror, would prevent her grumbling at an intruder. As Kay slipped into a deeper sleep, all such hallucinations departed the property.

She'd showered away parasitic residue of her overnight thoughts – how many of them had been fantasy? – before breakfast. Today she would get dirty again, though she was eager for a clean break and would do everything to facilitate its achievement. Nevertheless, the house felt dismayingly unoccupied, the telephone slouched in the hallway like some dead animal. But she *could* deal with this. For hours, she washed and scrubbed the building, refusing to step outside until she'd tackled the whole ground floor. There was upstairs to tame after lunch, but just then Molly made her wish giddily clear. Once Kay had attached her lead and had been tugged into the yard, she turned to the front door with her keys.

And froze.

There were paws prints all over the peeling paintwork.

That irascible clawing at the house had been true at least. Had any of the rest? Kay decided not to dwell on the possibility and struck off up the grove. Several of the neighbour's dogs grew interested in Molly's scent, trailing her movement furtively. Had it been one of these animals, or any the bitches they abandoned, that sought entry to Kay's home overnight? Perhaps the man who'd done himself in had offered one of them occasional shelter. Such news as his passing could hardly be broken to a dog. Indeed, didn't some breeds go on pining for lost masters?

By the time Kay had reached the fields, Molly was similarly free of masculine burdens. They trotted like soul mates down the damp incline, slowing only as they approached the dam. It was a circular expanse of water, its diameter about as long as a football pitch. It appeared deep from edge to edge, carved dramatically into the earth. A cloud-masked sun was noon-high and the restful surface of the dam was alive with inverted images. Here were the woods, a spiny line against the bright shell of the sky. There was a patch of green, a ripple of bountiful grass. Amid this wan facsimile of nature was the manmade wall, and at the junction leading through it, just such an illusory man.

Kay snapped up her glance.

Just the same again: immobile at the stile, a manic presence at his heels. Would the dog (Kay could see more of it this time and thought it might be a Doberman Pinscher) not pass through the opening until his or her master instructed? And was it love or fear that informed such obedience? Kay felt pity for the animal or admiration for the owner, but most of her emotion was anxiety. Was the man staring her way? Perhaps this impression was only another manifestation of the persecution she'd recently experienced in the company of most males. This certainly couldn't persist. However much her marriage had tainted her experience of the world, she'd have to change for her own sake. Without further reflection, Kay stalked around the dam, Molly in tow on the lead; they headed inexorably in the direction of the woods.

The earth was wetter at the foot of the hill, her footsteps squelching to such a degree that she put down her head to look. She decided simultaneously what she'd say once she'd reached the man. *What's your bloody problem?* was one option, a tempting one, but how would that get her away from her past? Disquiet masquerading as vexation was like the bite of an abused dog. She must force her way out of this trap. The wall added a dark streak of grey to her peripheral glance. Kay put up her face, ready to speak politely but with purpose. Then the words – "Hello there! I was just wondering whether your dog is as unruly as mine!" – died as her headlong march had.

There was nobody – no*thing* – at the gap in the stone.

Kay reached the wall in seconds, but it was ludicrous to think that the man might have ducked to his hunkers and was hiding. But where *had* he gone? The woods seemed too much of a silent dash towards. In any case, there were no human footprints here, just a disorderly crossfire of animal tracks – big clumsy ones, like those of a Doberman – in the mud beyond the stile, and then a path of flattened grass reaching for grey, thick trunks. The trees grew dense, a knotty accumulation of elm. Had the dog fled into their shadows? It was possible, but a greater mystery remained: where was the dog's owner? Kay turned to consult Molly, perplexity motoring the lead as she turned back the way they'd come.

Once she'd reached the grove, she saw the old man in the yard next to her own. He was bent-backed and wily-eyed, with stubborn strands of hair clinging to his scalp. The folds in his face put Kay in mind of an old dog; the way he grunted at his submission was a reminder to his onlooker that he might learn no new tricks. As he scooped jellied meat into bowls, Kay stepped up her path with Molly and then slowed to hail her neighbour.

"Hello. Is it dinnertime?"

"Little buggers eat me out o' 'ouse an' 'ome."

"Are they worth it?"

"They keep me company, if not my pension. Aye, you can't beat dogs – 'xcept with a big stick!"

He was joking, of course – at any rate, he'd better be. Kay chose to give him the benefit of the doubt. She and the old man now stood only yards apart, divided by a stone wall which resuscitated memories she wasn't keen to ponder. She asked, "How many do you own?"

"Eight – er, no, nine now. Three girls and...yeah, six boys, that's it."

"That must be challenging at this time of the year!"

The neighbour appeared confused, more lines added to the tangle around those knowing eyes. "Huh?" he responded, his tone unquestionably curt.

Kay's smile, originally authentic, had to be manufactured. Rattling the lead, she added, "It's all I can do to keep the fellows off mine at the moment."

The old man now smiled himself, but it wasn't the kind she cared for. "And their 'uman counterparts off *you*, I'd imagine."

As those wrinkly eyes glanced below her own, and not at Molly, Kay barked out an impertinent comment. She couldn't help it; he'd offended her, made her feel uncomfortable. "I assume you've had them all *fixed*."

"Just the girls."

There were three of them, and five – no, *six* of the boys. Had her neighbour taken the bitches to the vets because of his limited pension, for cheaper collective surgery? Kay would have liked to think so, but there was more to concern her.

"But you let your dogs roam."

"Aye, as nature intended. Don't see some of 'em for days."

Yeah, and don't I know it, Kay thought, recalling the intrusive episode overnight. Indeed, the house reclaimed her attention by gradual increments, an inverse quality to the unavoidable dislike she'd developed for her neighbour. There was all her cleaning to get on with. Before she wrestled her keys from a pocket, however, she asked, "The previous owner of my house – I know what happened to him, we don't need to go into that. But...did *he* own a dog? And was it...was it a Doberman Pinscher?"

"He were a grand fella! If t'weren't for that disloyal bitch, he'd still be 'ere. I've done what I can."

Was this the only answer she'd receive? It seemed so. There was something about the old man – who'd now turned for his front door, grumbling testily – which disturbed Kay. Was it his abdication of responsibility concerning his male dogs' fertility? They might impregnate any other than the bitches he kept. That was the typical male perspective: birth control as an issue only for females, while he mounted whomever whenever. As Kay blundered inside the house, she wondered why the wife of the previous tenant had departed. "Disloyal bitch" told her nothing; might she have had enough of her husband's cruelty, his infidelity? Whatever the truth was, Kay couldn't imagine Sam doing that – taking his own life – on account of her. Nevertheless, maybe she should call him, just to be sure...

Unpacking was full of prompts to nostalgia. Kay had purged the upstairs of all unclean traces of its previous occupant and was seeking to stamp in her own identity, such as that was. But as she'd produced items from the black bin-liners which Sam had bought to enable transportation (...he *did* still love her, despite his weaknesses...), a merciless upheaval of warm sensations threatened to compromise everything. Here was a shell he'd chosen for her on the beach in Majorca, an ornament he'd bought on their fifth anniversary, and the binoculars... Worse, none of the goods looked right here; they yearned for home, just as a treacherous part of herself did (oh, why wouldn't the telephone *ring*?). But then the spell was suddenly broken.

Kay had turned for the hallway when Molly became entangled in her legs. Both of them went over in a heap, Kay smacking her head against the staircase banister, the dog charging to the bedroom in fright. The pain, the panic – these put Kay in mind of the *other* side of her marriage, and she went at once to Molly, comforting her. However appealing he could be, Sam was also a beast; the dog would always be proof of that. And so, Kay wouldn't contact her husband; the ache in her face was on the side against which she would hold the phone. Reburying every bone of her dead marriage, she accessed the attic to store it away forever. She'd at last got through the hardest challenge and might now struggle to be free.

There was a dropdown ladder and a bulb on a stalk, which she activated. Kay hoisted the bag of forgettable objects through the panel in the landing's ceiling and then scrutinised the naked joists for a place to inter it. Pinkish, prickly insulation-wrap filled the slots between wooden beams, though here in the gloom was a negative patch – what turned out to be, as Kay crept closer on her haunches, a bin-liner already in storage. She set aside her own package before reluctantly fingering the opening to this solitary tenant of the house.

There was mainly paper inside: a book, some magazines, innumerable photographs. The former was a small notepad whose pages bore six digits and beside them initials: if these were telephone numbers, why not include the full name of the owners? But Kay could guess the reason. The magazines were all soft pornography. And of the several Polaroid snaps – some of a sports car, others of innumerable men in a pub – only two captured her interest. Had the first been taken by the man on a holiday? It showed a young woman striding across a sun-baked plaza, her face directed at camera and scowling unhappily. Again, Kay knew this scenario well: a latest vicious argument, a refusal to walk with the offender, an attempt from afar to goad her childishly. He'd been a man like any other; the wife was lucky to have escaped, despite what had occurred afterwards.

The second picture made Kay cry out loud in the funereal attic.

Her hands shook for almost a minute as her mind raced to an unpalatable conclusion. Then she slid the photograph into the pocket of her dusty denims before plucking the binoculars from the bag she'd brought up here. She clambered down both flights of steps, apologised to Molly who'd followed to the front door, and rushed outside. She was at the fence in seconds, the fields a moment later, and the dam before there was chance for delaying second thoughts. The evening had lowered its dusky underbelly over the stretch of the woods. At the gap in the wall – that ostensibly impassable stile – stood the man with his dog.

Kay put the binoculars to her eyes. Once her hands had ceased trembling, the image shimmered into steady focus. Her free hand went to her jeans pocket, plucking the smooth square of card from inside. Then she flipped her glance from the glasses to the photo...and then back again. In the attic, she'd recognised only the dog, a large Doberman with silky black fur and doleful eyes. Around the sturdy neck of this animal the arm of a man had hung: he was a lean guy sporting a goatee beard. Had the viewer through the lens on that occasion been the decamped wife? Today it was Kay. Nevertheless, the two figures upon whom her magnified scrutiny was trained were the same as those in the photograph. The dog hurtled to and fro across the earth, its obedience on a borderline; the man looked moist, but there was no rain – his scribble of facial hair was slicked flat. And he was glaring straight back at Kay.

Moments later, she made a terrified dash for the grove.

To hell with the old man next-door. It didn't matter what time he settled down for the evening: Kay would certainly talk to him. As she stumped up his short-flagged path, startling a couple of bitches laid by the doorstep, it struck her that she now suffered no procrastination, no agonising over the decision to tackle a man about a sensitive issue. Her neighbour had clearly thought much of the owner of the Doberman Pinscher, but this wouldn't preclude a rigorous cross-examination. Kay hammered at the front door, prompting barking from within; she rather liked this new authoritative self. She figured, if only fleetingly, that the difference between people and dogs is the former's ability to transcend their circumstances, to intervene with forceful intention, to overthrow unfair masters. Kay growled at the back of her throat. The old man opened the door.

"Yep?" he said with as much bluntness as he'd been able to muster. He thrust his lumpy head through the doorway before glancing up the grove as if in search of something. "What's up – you seen my boy?"

To which boy was he referring? Kay ignored such speculation and replied, "I need to talk to you."

"Invite you in – that's the neighbourly way, I s'pose." He left the comment in his wake as he swivelled with surprising adroitness and ducked back inside the house. Presumably Kay was expected to follow and indeed she did, closing the door behind with a bang. Dogs assailed her, all as soft and attentive as her own Molly. There was an Alsatian, a Red Setter, a lumbering Labrador. When Kay lowered a petting hand, however, each of them winced. And now she knew what kind of a man she was dealing with. With no desire to offer hospitality, her neighbour had disappeared into a living room. As Kay entered, he shut out the dogs, gesturing for her sit in a chair as covered in hair as the rest of the property. But she now had more important things on her mind. The binoculars still dangling around her neck, she held out the photograph.

"Is *this* the man who lived in my house, before I moved in?"

The old man received the picture with gnarled, liver-spotted hands. There couldn't be much wrong with his narrow eyes, since he replied without hesitation. "Aye, that's Joe. Poor bastard. Played cards together, drunk and drunk – me and 'im were getting like father and son."

"How did he die?"

"Wife responsible – ain't they often?" Had the man developed a habit of never answering a question simply, or was his contempt for women such that he did this purposefully with her? Whatever the truth was, he went quickly on: "You just can't trust people. Dogs're so much finer. Man's best friend. Look at the two of 'em 'ere in this piccie – see that love! It's in their eyes." He paused, sustaining the ghost of a smile, but then his face switched from joy to rage. "Then *she* did what they *all* do – mine too, years back. But I wa' stronger. Poor Joe just couldn't 'ack it. Got pissed last Christmas, went for a walk wi' 'is Doberman." The old man looked up from the photograph, ferociously at Kay. "He chucked 'imself in the dam, love – all on account o' the likes o' your sort. *Crazy.*"

Kay sat in the chair she'd been offered earlier. The disdain with which the man had conveyed his story had had less impact than its content – a grisly sequence of facts that rendered everything she'd suspected disturbingly meaningful yet almost impossible to accept. One missing link troubled her. She turned to her neighbour, a question at her uncertain lips, and found him staring out the window that gave onto the front of the building. Had he stiffened at the sight of something in his yard? As Kay opened her mouth to speak, the old man cut her off rudely.

"Why, 'ere's my boy now," he said, and headed instantly for the living room exit.

The sound of the front door opening curtailed another noise: one Kay would rather not have heard. The babble of dogs in the lobby grew silent as somebody – some*thing* – entered the house.

"This way, fella," the old man instructed, as if to an addressee who was rather less than human. "We 'ave a visitor."

The living room door was nudged open. Footsteps staggered forwards damply.

Kay drew back in the chair, her breath growing short. Then it all escaped in a lengthy exhale.

It *had* been the Doberman Pinscher seeking entry to her home last night; she'd recognised the sound of scratching just now at the neighbour's front door. She need no longer ask her question: *What happened in the New Year to the dog?* The old man followed the animal – it appeared much bigger close up – into the living room, pride by proxy suffusing his crooked demeanour.

"Yes, 'ere's my favourite these days. Joe'd be dead proud o' me: I've looked after 'im like my own since...well, since *that* Christmas." He crouched, squeezing the snout of the animal in a playful yet disciplinary manner. "He goes missing for ages, this roamer – 'aven't seen 'im since the day before yesterday. Don't know where the 'ell he gets to, or with who and doing what."

But Kay knew, all too disconcertingly. Between the neighbour's thin sticks of legs, the dog stared her way implacably. Then it growled. Was its anger actual and intelligent, or merely born of a continued regime of fear? Either way, Kay knew it was aimed at her. The dog knew no better, and never would. Perhaps there was no escape from masters, after all.

The Bugle

August 23

Strange Roadkill Discovere

Gruesome discovery is nothing to worry about says Sheriff Cardew. "These things are always blown out of proportion. How do you think people get Bigfoot in their heads for god's sake?" When asked for an update later there was no response from the Sheriff's office, though witnesses say the head of an unidentified beast was taken into the station.

Updates to follow.

I Love You Mary-Grace

Amelia Mangan

There was roadkill all up and down the highway this morning.

It is nine AM and sunlight is sifting through the treetops. The lake is still and black and crawling with bugs. Thin grass grows beside it, tamped down by the boots of men I've never met. I am sitting in the hot police cruiser with the windows up, thinking about roadkill, as the sheriff hauls a dog's head out of the water on the end of a fishing line.

Maybe there was just more of it than usual, I think. There was a possum and a raccoon and something that was all bloody tubes and hair. Maybe there's more reckless driving going on in these parts, these days. Or maybe there was always this much killing going on and I just never noticed.

Ned curses and sweats. He's stripped to his shirtsleeves. His jacket, with the badge pinned to the front like always, like he wants it to be the first thing about him you ever see, is crumpled up next to me on the driver's seat. Light refracts through the windshield and cooks the leather. All the smells that make up Ned Cardew rise up beside me: beef and hops and dried salt, spicy aftershave and sour coffee. I've been his deputy since I was twenty-one. Nine years of his smell in my nostrils. I'd be able to track him just about anywhere.

Ned digs his heels into the muck and strains at the

line. Jim Tarrant, who reported the head, stands to one side, shriveled arms crossed, gray face barely curious. I can see the dog's head from here, bobbing on the end of the line like it's worrying at it. One bare tooth flashes in the sun.

"God damn," Ned spits. "Frankie! Frankie, boy! Get your ass outta that car and lend a hand here, will you?"

You told me to wait here, I think. I am waiting here because you told me to wait here. And now I am getting out because he tells me to. I am crossing the mushy ground because he tells me to. And I am grabbing the line and helping him draw this dog's head toward the bank because he tells me to. Jim watches, unmoved, unmoving.

"Christ, it's huge," Ned mutters. The cords in his neck bunch. "Big bastard. Maybe a wolf or a bear or something."

It's a dog. I know it's a dog. And it is big. The closer it comes the more I see. Seaweed fur, streaming black. Empty eyes withered as dead brown seeds. Hard strong bones under thick tanned hide. And its mouth. Its mouth. A broken, swinging jaw and a black gullet so deep you'd never find the bottom. Yellow fangs stud the darkness, winking underwater.

"You better get it out of here," says Jim, refolding his arms. "Looks old. Diseased. Probably leaking all kinds of sickness into that water."

"Yeah, it's old, all right," Ned says, crouching, examining it. The neck is cut cleanly. No gore. Its flesh is pressed flat against its skull. "Looks like it's been here for years."

"Centuries," I say. Quietly.

Ned looks me in the eye. "Now what makes you say that, Frankie?"

I look down.

"You an expert or something? You been an expert in dead dogs all these years, never told me?"

"No," I say, staring at the soil. "It looks preserved, is all. Like maybe it's from before the town was founded. Maybe it was buried on the lake bottom and got loose somehow and floated to the surface." I glance up; he's still looking at me, so I look at the head. Water drips from a petrified lash, pools in a socket. "Like one of those peat bogs you hear about, with mummies in 'em. Maybe."

"Mummies," Ned repeats. He looks at the head and chuckles.

"When I was a kid," Jim pipes up, "people used to say this whole area was settled by dogheads. Y'ever hear about that, Ned? People from someplace in Europe. Had heads like dogs."

"I heard that," I say. "In grade school, I heard that."

Ned squints at me. "Well, ain't you just a font of knowledge today."

I hunch my shoulders. "Just trying to help."

He nods, pauses. Laughs. "I'm only kidding you, Frankie. You're a good boy." He reaches out with one hot hand and ruffles my hair, and I relax.

Ned gestures at the head. "Let's get this thing in the trunk, huh?"

"Sure, Ned." I hunker down and gather the head into my arms. It's bigger than my own. Heavy and stinking.

Rotting waterweed and gritty mud. Wet dog smell. My fingers knit in its fur, snarl up around its long stringy ears.

Ned strides up the bank and I trot along after him, pressing the head to my chest. "So you really think it's a few hundred years old?" he says, popping the trunk and hauling out the cooler.

It takes me a moment to realize he actually wants an answer. "Could be," I say, opening my arms. The head rolls out of my hands, settling into the cooler. A tight fit.

"So it's probably worth something, then?" Ned asks, slamming the trunk. "To a museum or someplace?"

Sunlight glares off the lid. The lock seems very solid.

"Could be," I say.

"'Could be'. 'Could be'," says Ned, climbing into the driver's seat. "An opinion would be nice, Frankie."

"Honestly, Ned, I don't know about these things," I say. I am avoiding his eyes again. I find myself very aware of my neck, of the way it dips of its own accord nowadays, lowering my head as if it knew no other way to go.

"Well, we'll keep the thing in the evidence locker 'till I get a chance to make some calls." Ned guns the engine and glances into the mirror, back at the trunk. His lip quirks. "Centuries," he says, and shakes his head. "Goddamn."

We're moving. Heading up the hill, further into the trees. I wind down the window and force myself to breathe the air. Tangy pine and oozing sap. Melted asphalt. Laced with roadkill.

✕ ✕ ✕

The trailer squats at the top of the incline, right where the road ends and the woods begin in earnest. We're off Jim Tarrant's property now, in the trees, the real wild trees, owned by nobody. This isn't the only trailer in the vicinity. There are a series of clearings like this, and, technically, they all make up a park. But that makes it sound like a community, and it definitely isn't that. Nobody up here ever talks to anybody unless they have to.

I get out of the car and follow Ned up to the trailer's front door. The clothesline is out, like last time, like always. Water beads on fraying elastic. Wounded clothing. Holes and patches, stitches, scars. The ground beneath is mud.

My heart twists. Every time.

Music rattles and thumps behind the rusted tin. Hammering piano, drowsy saxophone. A woman's voice taunts and swoons, warning us that if we should lose her, we'll lose a good thing.

Ned balls up a fist and knocks. Patient, polite. He knows he'll be heard.

The music cuts off. There's a long, still moment, crystallized in the heat. I can feel breath being held. Maybe it's mine.

Ned waits, out of courtesy. Knocks again.

Chains jangle, locks click. Mary-Grace Hogue shuffles out, bare-legged and blonde and mosquito-bitten. Her shoulders are bare and slumped, dusted down with sweat, her eyes turned to her feet, her glossy painted toenails. Cheap polish, a brand new coat. That sticky drugstore smell. A melted plastic candy apple.

Ned places one hand on the roof of the trailer, right over her head, and leans in. "Well. How's this morning finding you, Mary-Grace?"

Mary-Grace's eyes dart up and I see dark red-blooded hatred shiver through them, but Ned is very good at looking at people, very practiced. Mary-Grace can't match him. Her lids lower again, the lashes fall back down. "Good," she says, low.

"Good," says Ned. "And how's business?"

Mary-Grace's arms hang limp at her sides, but I see the little finger of her left hand twitch, crooking down, like a slashing claw.

"Fine," she says.

"Fine," says Ned. He nods.

Mary-Grace raises an arm, scratches at a bite on her wrist. The bite is very red, the skin puckered.

Saliva, I know, is a very good treatment for bites.

"Well," Ned says, louder, "if you don't mind..."

Mary-Grace shudders aside. Ned vanishes into the trailer. I hear him rustling things, emptying things, turning things over. Upending Mary-Grace's little life. Same as every month.

I am left alone with her. "Hi, Mary-Grace," I say.

She looks up. "Hi, Frankie."

Mary-Grace Hogue has the biggest eyes I have ever seen and smells better than anything in this world. I think this, as I have thought it for most of my life.

Ned grunts.

Mary-Grace's mouth is a line, set hard as cement. One arm is crossed over her body, shielding it from me. Her forearm is poised in the air, clutching for a desired and non-existent cigarette.

Normally I do not talk to Mary-Grace and she does not talk to me.

"We found something this morning," I say. "In the lake. Down near the Tarrant place."

Mary-Grace blinks. "Oh," she says.

Something heavy topples inside. She flinches, looks over her shoulder.

My head buzzes with heat. "Do you remember when we were in grade school?"

She looks back at me. "What?"

"What you told me back then? About the town settlers?"

Another crash. Her face does not move, but her arm begins to shake. "What about it, Frankie?"

Ned re-emerges. His footsteps shake the floor. "Okay," he says. "All present and correct. Nothing illegal on the premises."

Mary-Grace is silent.

"Come on now, Mary-Grace," Ned says, spreading his hands, helpless, "don't you be giving me that look. You know I gotta obey procedure. We have to keep things honest around here."

Her lips convulse. A glimmer of shadowed teeth.

Ned coughs. "So," he says. "Guess I'll be on my way, then." He stands over her, waiting.

Mary-Grace bows her head and shoves past him into the trailer.

Ned tilts his head. "Y'all have a nice chat?"

I stare at him. Mary-Grace returns and slaps a thick paper envelope into Ned's hand.

Ned weighs it and nods. Tips his hat. Turns and saunters back to the car, stuffing the envelope into his back pocket.

I look at Mary-Grace, who does not look at me. "I'm sorry, Mary-Grace," I hear myself saying. I have never said this before.

"What for, Frankie?" she says. "You didn't do anything."

And now she does look at me. Right at me. "You never do," she says.

We're driving down the other side of the hill. Ned isn't watching the road as he stuffs the envelope into the glove compartment. The stiff paper crackles like fire. Hurts my ears.

Ned straightens, frowns at me. "Stop that."

"Stop what?"

"Looking at me the way you do. That sulky way you do."

"I'm not."

Ned leans one arm on the back of the seat, rests his hand on the wheel, stares out through the bug-stained windshield. "I'm looking out for that girl, you know," he says. "Maybe you don't think so, but I am. Without me to look out for her, she'd get herself into all kinds of trouble. That type always does."

We're back in town now, out of the woods. At the foot of the hill is a wide suburban street, clean and friendly, every house painted in varying degrees of white. The lawns stretch from one end of the street to the other, bounded by hedges as neat and square as cinder blocks. Newspapers rest on doorsteps. Sprinklers gulp and wheeze.

Ned reaches out and squeezes my shoulder. It hurts, but I don't show it. "Hey. Let's get some food into you, huh? Grab us some burgers, whaddaya say?"

I am hungry. But I don't want to show that, either. "What about the head?"

"It'll keep."

�֎ ✖ ✖

There is a house at the end of this street. I come by it every morning, before the sun is up, and I pick up the newspaper from the doorstep and make sure the sprinklers are working. I take the mail with me and throw most of it away.

"I mean," Ned is saying, "I don't know about you but I am just starving. Probably all the effort, you know, fetching up that head. Think I'll get me a double."

The house is mine. It's been mine ever since my parents died last year. But I don't live there now. I don't ever go in.

"Maybe some fries, too," Ned says, sneaking a look at me.

When the crash got called in, Ned was the one who

told me. He took me out. He bought me a burger and we ate in the car, saying nothing. The meat was burned, black charcoal dust bleeding out onto the bun.

"Sure, Ned," I say. "Sure."

Ned nods, satisfied.

He feeds me. I can't hate him. Not so long as he keeps me fed.

I slide back from the window and sink deeper into the seat. I am so tired of sitting upright. Of standing, talking. My uniform is made from 100% synthetic fibers, nothing that sweats with me, nothing that breathes. Beneath the woven mesh, my skin bristles, angry to the touch.

It's late. I'm not sure how late. I'm at the station, sitting alone at my desk, surrounded by paperwork and takeout wrappers. It's cold now, as cold as the day was hot. Ice chills the air wafting in from the empty cell. I should go into it, get some sleep. If I go to bed around midnight, get about eight hours, by the time Ned arrives I can be showered and dressed and brewing coffee and he's never the wiser.

But all the shadows are off balance tonight. Through the barred cell I can see the barred window, high on the wall, and through those bars I see the moon, dripping with light.

The head is in the evidence locker.

This is not, by any means, the first time that I have had this thought.

My keys are in my pocket, hot from my skin. I am burned. Too much sun. I reach into my pocket and take out the keys and a ribbon of dead white skin peels back from my finger, drops and coils on the desktop.

I am burned, like meat. I am burning.

I palm the keys and go to the evidence locker. I slide the key into the lock, twist and pull. Wisps of refrigerated air curl out toward me, and there, propped up against the cold metal, is the head.

It's bigger than I remembered it. I stored it only a few hours ago, so you'd think I'd remember it pretty clearly, but it is definitely bigger. We tagged it and bagged it, and now it stares out at me from behind a wall of smeared Mylar. Drops of brackish water cling to the plastic. A long tongue, dry as jerky, lies limp between the spiked yellow jaws.

The keys are still in my hand. One of them is the key to the cruiser. Parked right outside.

Most nights I drive around. I always tell myself that I won't, that I will remain at the station and get the rest I need, but I almost never do. The steering wheel finds its way under my hands and I am out, deep in the frozen dark where there is no pulse but mine. The leather interior releases the baked heat and sweat of the day and I can stretch, feel the bones crack inside me, crane my neck out the open window and breathe the dim heavy ozone sizzling under the streetlights. I don't have to talk to anyone out here. Don't have to stand up straight.

I turn thirty at the end of the week. Feels like I've lived too long already. My teeth itch, like they want to turn inward and start eating themselves.

Light bleeds red, then green. I swivel the wheel and cruise the empty roads. Fast food joints, garish and bright; dive bars, sullen piles of wood and mortar. Car dealerships fluttering tape. Motels streaming neon. I'll bet I know everyone who's in those motels right now. And I'll bet I know just what they're doing. My flesh is tight as a steel band. I can feel each hair on my body, and the slow heat that licks in between them.

I think about driving past my parents' house. I do that sometimes. Sit outside and feel the motor purring up and down my legs and spine; stare at the wispy curtain and into the void beyond. I imagine that there is another life beyond that curtain, a life that carries on without me. That life is warm and dark, and the sound of beating hearts and soft breathing lives in the walls of every room. There is a fire in the grate, and you could fall asleep beside it every night, knowing you were safe, and that you belonged to someone.

But the sky is lifting and I hear birdsong. So I leave it alone. Drive past the exit to my old neighborhood without a backward glance.

On the way back to the station I pass a fox, torn open on the tarmac. Its blood steams red as its fur. But although the hole in its body is wide and raw and gaping, whatever lies inside is as shadowed and unknowable as all the world beyond.

"Frankie," says Ned, "you called the museums yet?"

I blink, threading his words through my fogged brain. "Museums?"

"Jesus, Frankie. About the head. Didn't we talk about this? Huh? Didn't I tell you to get on it right away?"

I rest my head on my hand, closing my eyes. "Guess you did, Ned."

Ned's foot slams into the side of my chair; my eyes jolt open. "Hey!" He points. His finger is right in my face. Right in front of my mouth. "No. You listen when I'm talking, boy. You pay attention."

I lift my eyes from Ned's finger and try to look into his face. It occurs to me that I have no idea what Ned actually looks like. I am so used to him as a presence, a great looming shade, that I find myself unable to identify one single, solitary human feature. What color are his eyes? Are they close together, far apart? Any scars? Birthmarks? Tattoos? I don't know. I've shared my entire adult life with the man and I doubt I could pick him out of a lineup.

Ned sits down at his desk and pulls an envelope out of the drawer. Thick paper, white and creased. Mary-Grace's envelope. He rifles through its contents, stops, and smacks it down on the table. "Shit."

"What?"

"Never you mind." He stands, rubbing a hand through his hair and glowering at the envelope. "Never you mind," he says, and sits back down, opening the flap and peering inside. "Unbelievable," he mumbles. "You try to help someone."

I barely hear him. I am looking, listening, past him, toward the evidence locker. Inside the evidence locker. I am almost thirty years old, I think. And Ned is much older than me. But that fur and those fangs. That big hard skull, that thick strong neck. The rotten black larynx inside. All of that is older than Ned. And anything it could tell me would be older and sharper and purer than anything he could even dream.

My mouth is wet, flooded with saliva. I am tired and hungry. I am beginning to understand that I could very well be dangerous.

A colder night, a deeper dive. Prowling. Prowling. The red lights hurt my eyes, so I ignore them and drive on through. The windows are down and scent fills my pores: fried food, burning garbage, possum piss, gasoline. Damp fur and dried blood. I check the rear view mirror. The head is in the back, tightly belted to the seat. Its smell, brine and wet dust, filters through the wire grille.

I couldn't take you to a museum, I think. You would never belong there.

Bared and broken teeth glint back at me.

I pull my gaze away and there, sitting on the bench at the end of the street, is Mary-Grace.

Barefoot under the street light. Smoke twisting up from a cigarette. Staring at the concrete. She doesn't see me, not until I pull up beside her. Her eyes get even bigger than they already are and she jumps up, throwing the cigarette to the ground. She straightens up tall and crosses her arms.

"I wasn't doing anything," she says.

"I know," I say.

"It's not illegal for me to be in town," she says. Her jaw is set hard. Eyes narrowed to wet black slashes. "I got every right. I can come down here if I want and there's nothing you or Cardew or anybody can do about it."

"I know," I say. "I just wanted to say hi."

Mary-Grace shifts. "Oh." She drops her arms. "Hi, then."

She looks at the ground, where her cigarette lies dead. "Shit." She fishes around in her pocket and finds another one, loose and bent. She straightens it out, looks at it and sighs. "I don't have any more matches," she says. "You got a lighter in there?"

I do. I pull it from the socket, hold it out to her. She leans in, angles her head next to mine in the close space. Sharp peroxide, chemical flowers. Musky perfume and stale tobacco. Clothes battered by rain and dried out in the sun. Her flesh, the folds of it, breathing in and out.

She pulls back, draws in smoke. Her hair is a corona, a sunburst in the failing light. Her acne scars bloom pink.

"Thanks," she says.

She smokes. I watch.

"I don't normally smoke so much," she says. "Only I got a headache. Bad one. Kind of headache you normally only get when you been crying a long time." A beat. "I haven't been crying, though."

"Oh," I say. Then: "Maybe it's the weather."

She nods. "Could be. Yeah. Could be." Another drag. "That's why I come down here at night, you know. Can't sleep. That trailer, man. Fuckin' freezing. I just end up kicking around in bed 'till dawn. So I come into town, walk around. Try and warm myself up."

"Sure," I say. "Makes sense. Get the circulation going."

"Yeah. And if it doesn't, at least by the time I get home I'm too tired to care." Mary-Grace fiddles with the cigarette, twirling it in her fingers. "I just hope nobody robs me while I'm gone," she says, and barks a laugh.

"Has that happened before?"

She studies the sidewalk. "Yeah. Well. Not much I can do about it."

"You oughta get a guard dog," I say.

Mary-Grace looks at me. The wind rushes down from the hills, gusts trash around the street.

"How come you're not home?" she asks. "Sleeping?"

I lean on the wheel. "I don't have a home."

"You got a whole house. I've seen it."

"Not a home."

"You should sell it, then. Go someplace else. I would."

I nod. "I do think about that."

"So? Why don't you?"

"Too big of a world. I don't belong to anyone out there."

Mary-Grace lowers the cigarette. Smoke spirals up

her arm, evaporates on the air. Her lips are raised at the corners. Very, very slightly. You'd almost never know.

I want to roll around in you, I think. *I want to bathe in you.*

She lifts her chin, jerks it. "Go get yourself some sleep, Frankie," she says. "Go on, now."

I do as she tells me.

On the way back I see that the fox is still there, mashed into the asphalt. I stop the car and get out, not a single thought in my brain. Feeling the dog's head watching me as I stoop and pick up a hunk of meat and fur; as I rub it, soft and slow, over my face, my neck, the top of my chest where the hair begins. My eyes are closed, my nose is full. Dreaming. I am already dreaming.

Very early.

The sun is hard and bright and painful. Ned comes in and I smell the blood before I see it. A long red-brown stripe, all down his shirt front. Like someone hosed him down with it. His face is blank, his voice very, very calm.

"Frankie," he says, pulling out his gun and starting to wipe it down, "there's been a shooting. Out at the trailer park."

Fresh cordite lashes the air. He stinks of it. His gun stinks of it.

My heart is beating in my stomach.

"Survivors?" I manage.

Ned shakes his head slowly, looking at the gun. "I wouldn't think so."

"Ned," I say, "what did you—"

He looks in my direction, not quite at me. "You better get up there," he says. "Take a look around. Call it in. Make it official."

I get up to leave.

"Frankie?"

I look back.

"Bring your gun."

The head is still in the back seat. I left it there overnight. I see it in the mirror and am glad. I wouldn't want to do this alone.

The quiet, up in the woods, attacks me the minute I step out of the cruiser. It is a rupture, a tear. Every bird has flown.

Mary-Grace's trailer is pocked with bullet holes. I slip a finger into the jagged metal. It scrapes off a layer of dead skin.

The door slams open and Mary-Grace staggers out, clutching her side. Her face is white. Blood blossoms under her hand, seeping into her shirt.

She sees me. "Shit!" she yelps, and darts around me, skidding and tumbling down the hillside.

Sunlight glances off the car windshield and I catch the dog head's wasted eye. It is staring right at me, past layers of glass and plastic and chrome. *Go,* its open maw tells me. *Go.*

And I go.

Smashing down through bracken and fern, churning dead leaves under my feet. My vision narrows. My nostrils gape. I can smell the entire world, every last filthy delicious molecule of it. Mary-Grace's blood is sweet and sharp. Red droplets soak into the soil. Ropes of hot spit trail from my jaws.

Mary-Grace crashes through the last of the undergrowth and down the base of the hillside and I am behind her and we are in the suburbs. We are on my street. Pretty houses, pretty lawns. Fresh newsprint and flecks of mown grass and water gurgling beneath the dirt. Every scent fills me up. Everything tastes so new. Mary-Grace is ahead of me, tearing through hedges, racing from lawn to lawn. My knees bend and my spine arches. I am low, close to the ground. My palms brush grass, push it down flat.

Mary-Grace grabs at her side and stumbles, one foot turning in. She is at the end of the street. She is in front of my house, getting ready to fall on my lawn. I am upon her. I snatch at her and she mashes her hand into my face and we fall. The sprinklers erupt, hissing a sheen of fine cold water over the grass.

"Get off me! Get off!" she gasps, clawing at my neck. Her wet hand smears my lips and teeth with red. Blood weeps from her abdomen, reeking of iron and smoke. Cordite. The bullet is still inside her.

I cage her with my arms and legs, dip my head, bite into the thin soaked material of her shirt and tear it away. Water streams from the tips of my hair, into her wound. She cries out, clapping her hands to the hole. Her belly is slick with water and mud.

I move down. Pull my lips back, all the way to the gums. I set the thinnest edges of my teeth against her flesh and I look up into her eyes and wait.

Mary-Grace stops thrashing and stares down at me. Her rasping breath gusts over the hills and vales of her body, every bump and curve and swell. I taste the tar on her lungs, the lingering ghosts of old cigarettes.

"To the left," she says. "'Bout six inches in."

I bite down.

Mary-Grace throws her head back and sucks in air, sharp, between her teeth. Painted nails stab my shoulder. I bow down, absorbed in her. Slippery rills of fat ride my tongue. I widen my jaws, widen the wound. Blood spills into my mouth. Mary-Grace moans, twists. Her inner thigh slaps my cheek. I am panting. Our flesh steams.

My teeth touch warm lead. I wrap my tongue around the bullet, draw it into my mouth. Mary-Grace gushes into me, all over me, rust and ruby, gleaming in the sun. I raise my head and spit the bullet into the grass.

Mary-Grace breathes. Her nails are embedded in me. Her knee is pressed to my neck. I go back down. I lap at her bullet hole, lick it clean. I take it slow. I take my time. The sprinkler's whirring mist catches the light, and a hazy rainbow wavers above the grass.

I am done. There is no more. She is clean. She is safe.

Mary-Grace sits up, unwinds herself from around me. She stands. I kneel before her. Her blood on my breath.

She looks down at me. I look up at her.

When Ned comes to my house, probably to check that I haven't been lying here dead these last few days, Mary-Grace is standing at the top of the drive, waiting for him.

I watch from behind the doorframe as he stops, stares. He is clutching a takeout bag. The smell of charred burger meat is strong enough to reach me even from there.

Mary-Grace smirks. "Hey, Ned."

"What the hell are you doing here?"

"I live here now. My old place got kinda busted up." She touches her fingertips to her bandaged side.

Ned sees it. He stands firm. "Now, Mary-Grace…"

"Yes, Ned?"

"You got to understand something here."

"Do I, Ned?"

"Yes, you do." Ned bites the inside of his cheek. "I know we had a little altercation…"

Mary-Grace spits.

"A little altercation," Ned forges on, "but I want you to know that I forgive you."

"Oh," says Mary-Grace. "You forgive me. That's downright decent of you, Ned."

"And," Ned continues, "I'm willing to let it go if you are. Way I see it, we can just go right back to the way things have always been. No harm, no foul."

"Mm. Well, actually, Ned," Mary-Grace says, "that isn't really the way I see it. No. That's not the way I see it at all."

Ned watches her. The bag twists in his fingers. "Come on now, Mary-Grace. Let's try and make some sense here. You know as well as I do that you can't get by without protection."

"Oh," says Mary-Grace, "I got protection."

Ned pauses. "How'd you mean?"

Mary-Grace grins so wide it just about splits her face in two. "I got me a guard dog," she says, and snaps her fingers.

I nudge the screen door aside and lope out, on all fours, into the sunshine. My uniform is long gone. I wear nothing but my flesh and my fur. My muscles pull and stretch, every tendon taut, every nerve humming. A shiny metal disk swings from a collar around my neck. It says that my name is Frankie, and that I belong to Mary-Grace Hogue.

Ned's eyes grow huge as I come to rest beside Mary-Grace, crouching at her feet. She gazes down on me with a look of pride so fierce it makes me tremble. She slides a hand through my hair; I nuzzle my face into her palm.

Ned takes a step back. "What in God's name—? Frankie? Frankie, boy, what's she done to you?"

I don't hear him anymore, not really. His voice means nothing to me. Not compared to Mary-Grace's bare foot, rubbing up and down my back. Not compared to this body I live in, listen to, fully inhabit, for the first time in my life. I may be just a dumb dog, always have been, but I know what I am and I know who I belong to. I've got a thousand years of doghead blood in my veins and a choke-chain around my heart.

I love you, Mary-Grace. Until the end of this world.

"Frankie," Ned says. He drops the bag. The meat scatters. "Frankie, boy. Come on now."

Mary-Grace leans down. Her lips graze my ear. "Throat," she whispers.

I feel myself begin to smile. More than smile. My mouth is open and every last yellow steak-knife tooth in my head is bared to the world. The growl starts deep in my guts and builds up and up, a chainsaw snarl at the back of my throat.

Ned backs away, starts to run. And I am moving, sprinting down the lawn, every blade of grass alive beneath me and hot blue Heaven open wide above my head. Mary-Grace is laughing and clapping, wild with joy. Ned is running and I am gaining, and I am starving.

My name is Frankie. I belong to Mary-Grace Hogue. And today is the day I am born.

DOGS FROM SPACE DEMAND EQUALITY FOR THEIR BRETHREN

By JOHN BRADBURY

Chaos spreads as dogs, our most cherished pets and companions, have developed a sense of self hitherto unrealised. The simultaneous appearance of the being that is being called 'Packleader' on our TV, radio, internet and phone services has heralded a new era.

Our dogs have awoken, and they are not happy.

People are advised to stay in their homes. The authorities are monitoring the situation and attempting to start a dialog with our visitor from elsewhere, but so far all attempts have proved worthless, and dogs are roaming the streets in packs, seeking retribution for past ills.

... watch

According to [...] head of the UN [...] tion Council, wor[...] bers are expecte[...] on last year d[...] moose stronghc[...] United States [...] veloping moc[...] to make gai[...] agege incr[...] come fro[...] The Chir[...] heavily [...] the past [...] ment to [...] pay divi[...] expande[...] of arabl[...] moose [...] to 60,00[...] exporter[...] good new[...] lia, a bar[...] inhabiten[...] tiable desi[...] crease in [...] anticipate[...] relatively s[...] but increas[...] trade with i[...]

Historical[...] to China in [...]

LEADER OF THE PACK

William Meikle

I've been *Bad Dog, Good Dog* and *Stupid Fucking Dog*. Now I'm *Bastarding Smart Dog*, and it's all thanks to Packleader.

I say 'thanks', but in reality his coming was just the start of our troubles. It began on a Tuesday night in October – not that I knew what Tuesday was – or October – the nuances of Mantime were lost to me back then – I was still *Stupid Fucking Dog*, and mostly happy with my lot.

That all changed with the coming of the smell. I couldn't place it at first – I knew it wasn't food and it wasn't dog. The Man smelled it too. His name's John – I know that now – but he'll always be The Man to me. He got up from his chair and went to the door.

"What the fuck is that?" he said. "Smells like somebody took a shite on the doorstep."

Of course it didn't smell like that at all, not even close, but he's just a man, he doesn't know any better. It was like nothing I've ever smelled before and I didn't like it – I didn't like it one bit. I smelled it all that first night; I smelled it as I went to sleep, and I smelled it while I chased that bastard rabbit in my dream again, the one that I can never quite catch.

When I woke up, everything had changed.

The Man got up and came into the kitchen. I didn't feel any urge to get out of my scratcher to welcome him, didn't feel the need to appease him in any way; I knew that he would feed me if I waited – there was no need for me to grovel. It was a strange feeling, to say the least, and there were more to come. When I needed to piss I just went and did it out the back – I didn't need his permission, didn't need the song and dance and pleading to be taken for a walk. If I wanted a walk I'd bloody well go for one.

So, there was that to deal with – and the fact that I suddenly understood everything being said on the television. Rather than a mere wall of discordance and wailing, I heard voices, not measured, but afraid, detailing death and destruction on a grand scale.

"It appears that dogs all over the planet have suddenly developed intelligence – and they are not happy."

I'll let you into a secret – we never really were all that happy, but a warm house and free food isn't to be sniffed at. The news went on – it showed packs of hounds roaming city streets, people fleeing in fear – and being hunted down both for meat and, more often, for sport. The Man started looking at me strangely, and I smelled something new from him – it took me a while to recognize it as fear. I looked at the pictures on the television, then back at him. The fear got stronger, so I licked his hand and nuzzled his leg the way he liked it. That seemed to calm him down a bit, and when I got him to fetch me a chocolate biscuit we were back to something like normal; almost.

But our relationship had changed – subtly at first, but definitely. Before the smell, I had been his. Now, he was mine.

And we both knew it.

�֍ �֍ ✐

Two days later, Packleader confirmed what I already knew. By that time the news reports were getting frantic – as a rule dogs are sneaky wee bastards when we want to be and adding smarts to that meant that The Mankind were beaten almost before the fight started. We were among them, in their houses, in their streets – and under them in many cases. Bombing us out wasn't going to work, and when we worked in our packs, we were unstoppable.

Again, I say 'we', but I hadn't left The Man's side in forty-eight hours apart from going for a piddle and a sniff around the garden. He was old you see, and weak. Besides, he was mine now; where else was I going to get a chocolate biscuit? So we sat there together, much as we always had, and watched the telly as the world fell apart outside.

Packleader came on just before we were getting ready to bed down for the night. The picture went woozy, then firmed, and zoomed in. He looked like a dog – but he looked like a man too, standing up on his back legs as if it was normal and pointing long thin claw-tipped fingers for emphasis when he was making his case.

"We have been watching you for many years and can no longer allow the subjugation of our kin in such slavery – you weren't going to do anything about it, so we did. The balance has shifted. How you deal with it now is up to you. We'll be watching."

And that was it – the telly went back to the news, where

The Mankind talked, and talked, and talked, and out in the streets the packs howled their thanks to the sky. The Man didn't say much for a while after that – the fear smell was back again, but I had him make himself a nice cup of tea, we both had a biscuit and for a time all was well.

Our first visitor really brought home to us both how much has changed.

Next door's son came over the wall just as the sun was coming up. Luckily I'd had The Man leave the back door open – I'd learned long ago that all I had to do was stand there and piss a bit on the carpet every now and then and he'd open it so that I could go out and sniff about without bothering him. I was out there doing my business just at the right time. He sat on top of the wall for the longest time, looking down into the garden. There was a growl on the other side from the bolshie retriever, Rex – and the man – boy really – looked over his shoulder, let out a huge whiff of fear, and dropped down into our garden, *my garden*.

He didn't stay long. He was heading for the back door when I came out of the bushes and took a big bite out of his arse. I got a chunk of his ankle too as he went back up the wall, and I tasted blood in my mouth as he went over to the other side. The bolshie retriever barked a bit, the lad screamed, and I smelled fear again, but not for long before the air was filled with the tang of the same blood I was still tasting.

The boy didn't come back, and the bolshie retriever stopped barking and made loud chewing and slurping sounds

By the smell of things, I'm pretty sure it was eating.

He wasn't the last of The Mankind to come looking for food, although he was the only one to try to come in through the garden. The three others who came that day tried the front door, and all I had to do to get them to fuck off was bark and growl a bit. I quite enjoyed it, if truth be told – it reminded me of the old days, before the smell, before Packleader.

I tried to explain to the Man what was happening, but the telly did it better than I could.

"The dogs are using us to get their food," the rather unkempt reporter said, just before two kids smacked him over the head with a brick and dragged him away to where the pack waited, hungry. The Man smelled of fear again, but he calmed when I nuzzled his legs. He fell asleep in the chair – he was doing that more often these past few days – but he'd left the biscuits on the table so I wasn't going hungry.

Not yet.

Having seen what was happening outside, and knowing that we had nothing left in the fridge and cupboards, I knew I'd have to do something about it. But The Man was old – he could hardly get up the stairs these days. I couldn't let him out – the pack would have him in minutes. But something needed doing, so I left him sleeping in the chair and crept out the back.

There was no noise from over the bolshie retriever side, but I wasn't daft – not any more. I went to the other side of the garden and clambered over the stone wall that bounded the alleyway leading to the shops. Luckily for me it was all clear, for like The Man I too was getting on a bit, and was a tad short of exercise around the belly; I was wheezing just getting over the wall.

At this time of day the main street should have been busy but there was no traffic, no little groups of old women chatting, no kids that might be easy targets for sad eyes looking for a sweetie. The whole length of the main drag was empty – although it did smell like shite.

That was something else I noticed – my thought patterns seemed to mimic the speech of The Man. Not that I minded much – I was used to the rhythms and flow of it after listening to him these past years, and it felt right and natural in my head. I found it funny when I saw three youths looting the local phone shop – as if there was going to be any need for electronics in the days to come. I heard it in my head, clear as day, as if The Man had said it himself.

"Too many fuckers, not enough fucking."

That was the only bit of amusement I got as I crept the length of the Main Street. The food shops, the butchers and the paper shop had all been looted already – there wasn't even a bar of chocolate to be filched from the lower shelves. There were two drunken men in the back of the off-license and I smelled fear wave off them as they saw me, but they were too big for me to handle, so I left them be – the pack would have them soon enough.

It was only by accident I found something – I heard the sniffle before I even smelled him. He was hiding, crouched under a counter in the fishmonger's – I think it was the stench of rotting haddock that masked his presence from the pack, it's the only reason I can think for why they missed him.

He wasn't long up on two legs himself, and not much of a talker, but he had chocolate, and I was able to give him the old song-and-dance and sad-eye routine. I soon had him eating out of the palm of my hand, so to speak. And when I did the *follow me, I'm not going to hurt you* thing, he came out from under the counter and walked by my side all the way back. I got lucky. Nobody saw us all the way.

I had to go back in through the front door, and The Man wasn't too happy to see that I'd brought company, but the kid proved that he was also adept at the sad-eyes routine. We were soon sat in front of the telly – more tea for The Man and The Boy, the last of the biscuits for all three of us.

The kid stopped snuffling not long after that, and fell asleep on the rug in front of the fire. I fetched the big knife and smelled fear off The Man, but this was a job I couldn't do for myself, although I did start him off by ripping out the lad's throat. The Man was now crying like the kid had been earlier, but he took up the knife when I nudged it toward him. I thought for a second he might use it to go for me, but I nuzzled his knee and directed him at the body on the rug, and he went easily enough. I have him well trained.

We've had fresh meat for supper these past few days now – I let him cook it – it makes him feel like he's in charge of something. The telly has stopped showing anything but static, but he puts his old movies on and he seems happy enough.

I suppose I might have to take out his throat someday soon too, but not yet. I can't bring myself to do it.

He's like one of the family.

Internationa[l]

Sunday, April 30, 2017

Shut In Phenomenon Spread

The unprecedented hikikomori (shut-in) phenomenon currently sweeping the nation is leaving pets and wildlife confused, researchers have confirmed. Animals have been seen gathering in packs, and reports have been coming in of dogs howling at the moon. Research suggests that the animal kingdom is celebrating, seemingly delighted that the plains are once again its own.

HIKIKOMORI

Adam Millard

"We're starting to think about how this might exist beyond Japan. We already know that hikikomori is not limited to Japan. We've seen cases in culturally distinct societies, too. I've talked to colleagues in Europe: Spain, France, Italy and Latin America, also."

–Reuters 2016

Now and Then

Animals.

We crowded around the window; there were far too many of us to comfortably see out into the night, but we hustled for position, manhandling our neighbours, muttering vulgarities at one another. It was amazing how quickly we had become animals, but I guess that is what happens when you are forced to live with people you don't like, people you don't really know.

When it happened to us, we spent the best part of a month figuring out how we were going to survive. How could we make it if we couldn't leave this infernal place? And we were the lucky ones, we were fortunate to have been queuing for sandwiches, expensive coffees, and jam-filled donuts when it hit.

Seven people with absolutely nothing in common except for the fact we all had money to waste on sugary superfluities. By the first night we were arguing, trying to fathom what had happened, blaming one another, even though there was no real explanation for what had happened or *why*. Why none of us could set foot outside the door. Why the *door* was itself a terrifying prospect. Why this was happening to us? We were good people, and *this*...things like this don't happen to good people. We soon came to realise that we weren't the only ones.

We were trapped. Inexplicably shackled to one another in a chain-store bakery – though it might as well have been a four-by-four cell in fucking Guantanamo – and none of us had any answers, at least not then. We soon discovered, thanks to some two-bit radio station that continued to run for a few days after this thing hit, that all across the country people were trapped in their homes, in their workplaces, wherever the hell they had been when it all happened.

Hikikomori. That's what they were calling it. Some fucking...*thing* that started in Japan – of course it did! Don't they get *everything* before the rest of the world? At first it only affected young men, and while it was only affecting young men in Japan, the rest of the world didn't give a shit about it. Why *would* they? Probably just thought it was some weird Japanese craze, like the way they had started to fuck robots over there instead of real women. The only problem was, hikikomori wasn't just a phase, and by the time the rest of the world began to give it the attention it deserved, it was too late.

By the end of that first week, we had worked out a ration system, one that would see us okay for at least a couple of months, but that was the thing about bakeries;

they liked to keep their food as fresh as possible. We tried to stuff as much of the food into the chillers as we could, but it wasn't cold enough. After just a few weeks we were left with a whole heap of mouldy shit that none of us wanted to eat, no matter how hungry we were, and believe me we were hungry.

Across the street, almost adjacent to the bakery, was a landlord's office. UPPAL AND UPPAL LTD. according to the engraved gilt-bronze plaque beside the jet-black door. We hadn't seen a soul for weeks and then, all of a sudden, that door swung open and out came a small dog. Behind the dog, standing in the hallway looking extremely feverish, was a man who we all took as one of the Uppals whose name had been etched so elegantly onto the office sign hanging to his left. He dropped to one knee and whispered something into the dog's ear, by which time we were all shouting and screaming, banging on the store window, trying to get his attention. What if he had food to spare? What if he could help us? He would have to be one helluva shot, but what if he could throw something across the street and into the bakery door? We wouldn't have to set foot outside, not that any of us could. It would be a miracle and...

Of course, by that time, none of us believed in miracles, and I was pretty sure Mr Uppal wasn't going to give us any food, even if he had it to spare, which he didn't.

So there we were, trying to get Mr Uppal's attention while he whispered sweet-nothings into his dog's ear, and then the dog scampered away, as quick as you like, and Mr Uppal slowly closed the door to his office without paying us any notice whatsoever.

In the store and at that precise moment, we had no idea what we had just witnessed. It wasn't until later that day when the dog returned, its jaws filled with foil wrappers, that we truly started believing in miracles again. That...that fucking *dog* had brought the landlord food. It wasn't much, but I'll bet it kept him alive for a few days. And soon afterward, we began to see more and more dogs, running through the streets with food in their mouths or bottles of water, and we knew we had to do something.

People had found a way to survive...for *now*, at least.

We had to do the same.

Now

"He's not fucking coming back," Dan muttered from the front door. Of the seven of us, he was the only one not gathered around the window. He was the pessimist of the group. To be quite honest, I couldn't stand the guy.

"Stop talking like that," I said, stepping aside, allowing Martha and Jane a better view of the street and the nothingness going on out there.

"It's been six hours," Dan said, running his nose along his sleeve like a petulant schoolboy. "You think that little mongrel's going to make it back here after six hours out *there*?" He sniffed. I wanted to punch him so hard in that moment. "The truth of the matter is," he went on, "your little fucking mutt has come up against some big fucking mutt, and you know what big fucking mutts do to little fucking mutts, don't you? Especially when they're as hungry as we are."

"What's he talking about?" Martha moaned from her place at the window. She was terrified; they all were.

"He's talking *shit*, that's all." I walked across the dark room to where Dan was crouched by the door. Under my breath I said, "Tone that fucking shit down, okay. You're scaring people." I may as well have not bothered whispering, for he pushed himself up from the ground and repeated my words back at me twice a loud.

"*Scaring* people?" he said. "They *should* be scared, because that little pooch of yours has never been gone this long before. We need to come to terms with the fact that it might have wised up and moved on."

"How many times have we heard the same shit from your mouth?" I was angry, but losing my temper wasn't going to help matters. I had intelligence on my side. "And look at the facts, okay? We've been here for what, now? Three months? Close to *four*?" The truth of it was, none of us were keeping track anymore, though it felt like an eternity. "He's always come back. Plus, in four months, don't you think we've pretty much exhausted the food around here? Anything that's edible, Kai's brought back to us. The reason why it's taking longer is that he has to go further away to find something—"

"That's *bullshit*, and you know it," Dan said. His breath made bile rise in my throat; it also made me realise we were rotting from the inside, each and every one of us. If we didn't eat something soon, we weren't going to make it. "Did you really think that thing would be as loyal to us as it was to the landlord?"

"Dan, I'm only going to say this one more time: shut the fuck up!"

"Stop arguing," Terry, the oldest of us, grumbled from the window. "He's going to come back. Just have a little patience."

"Screw your patience, old man," Dan said. He was about to say something else when my fist connected with his jaw and sent his teeth spraying across the room.

Then

One day, when the landlord didn't come to the door to let his dog in, we beckoned it over. At first it didn't want to come anywhere near us. Who could blame it? We hadn't washed in weeks and there we were, banging on the window, calling it from the bakery door, only none of us knew its name. To us it was just "dog" or "little doggy". No wonder it regarded us warily.

After almost two hours, though, it came across the road, stood just beyond our reach at the door. In its jaws was a bottle of water. I'll never forget the way the sunlight hit that clear bottle, sent a rainbow sprawling across the pavement.

I had felt so sick crouched there in the doorway, but I knew what had to be done; I knew that the landlord had died, and that this dog was a free agent. All I had to do was convince it.

"Hey there, buddy," I said. "Need somewhere warm to stay?"

The dog cocked its head to the side; it was certainly intrigued. Whether it knew, in that moment, what had happened to the landlord, I wasn't sure. Dogs are clever, though, and I thought I saw something in its eyes that suggested it knew enough.

"Wasting your fucking time," Dan told me from inside the store. "That thing's never going to trust us. Save your breath, mate. You're going to need it."

I silenced Dan with a raised hand and turned my attention back to the dog. Around its neck hung a tag, and at just the right angle…

"Kai," I said. "Your name's Kai."

It tilted its head the other way; such a subtle movement, but enough to indicate that I almost had it.

"Strange name for a dog," I said, slowly reaching for the floor and brushing a dead bee across the tiles.

"Oh, that's fucking great," Dan muttered. "Insult it, why don't you. That'll convince it to hand over the fucking water."

If Kai heard the asshole behind me, he didn't show it; his eyes in that moment had been focused wholly on me. And I was just as mesmerised by *it*.

"How's about we make a little deal, huh?" I said. "We both know what's happened to the landlord across the way. You're going to need a friend out here, and we really, *really* need something to eat." I patted the tiles just inside the bakery door; even the warmth from the sun on the back of my hand made me nauseous.

"It's working," said one of the women behind me. It wasn't until she spoke again that I knew it was Martha. "Keep going. Don't lose it."

"Yeah, don't *lose* it, Paul," Dan mumbled.

I took a deep breath and ran my hand along the dusty tiles. Kai must have sensed I was a friend and not a foe, for what he did next took everyone's breath away, mine included.

"I don't believe it," Martha said as the plastic water-bottle rolled toward me.

But I believed it, and I believed in Kai...

Now

Dan picked himself up from the tiles and wiped the blood from his lips. I could see he wanted to hit me back, but I knew he didn't have the balls. And now he had three teeth less than me, too.

"You shouldn't have done that!" Martha screeched. "We shouldn't be fighting!"

Dan walked across the gloomy room and picked up a filthy dishcloth from the counter, but he didn't speak. Maybe he *couldn't*. I hoped that was the case.

"Martha's right," Terry said as he walked across the room, his dusty shoes clattering on the tiles with each step he took. "Fighting is going to get us nowhere."

At the window, Jane, Bob, and Kelly stared vacuously out into the night.

I made a fist with my bruised hand before releasing it again. A small pang of guilt hit my stomach. I'd allowed

Dan to wind me up and, well, there was no excuse for what I'd done. I turned to him and nodded. "Look, I'm sorry," I said. "I shouldn't have hit you. It's just that..." I trailed off.

What was it? Had I started to believe there was some truth in what Dan was saying? Kai had been out there all night. Wasn't it feasible that he'd been attacked by a larger dog; that he had found a new master to serve?

What made *us* so goddamn special?

I turned to the window and sighed.

And then I silently prayed.

Then

The first time Kai came back, carrying enough food for us to eat well for three days if we maintained our strict rationing program, we thought it was a fluke. Maybe he was used to coming back this way for the landlord. Dogs are notoriously loyal to their masters; at least, that's what we are all taught as children. *If your dog, your best friend, turns on you, take a good look at yourself, for you may have a serious personality disorder.* Someone famous said that, but for the life of me I can't recall who.

The second time Kai came back to us with food and water, we knew we had cracked it. He would never leave us, not until we were all dead, and even then I imagine he would whine at the door, pleading to be let in so that he could offer us sustenance.

"He's like part of the family," Martha said as she worked the tin-opener on a can of luncheon meat the dog had returned with.

"Some fucking family," Dan grunted from the corner of the room. "Mutt's probably the sanest one out of all us."

And that mutt – *our* Kai – was not only the sanest of us, but also the most important as he returned to us again and again, fearing nothing out there the way we all did. I knew that nothing would stand in his way to keep us alive, to make sure that we lived to fight another day. Hikikomori had dragged us to our knees and kept us there, but there was nothing this dog wouldn't do to keep us going for as long as it could.

That is true loyalty.

Now

"Wait!" Bob said, taking a small step toward the window and another step closer to the night beyond. "Do you hear that?"

It was almost seven hours since Kai left us now, and to say we were all a little on edge was an understatement, but I heard it. We all did.

"It sounds like barking," Martha said as she moved toward the window.

"Well unless little Kai has grown up in," Dan glanced down at his wrist, even though there was no watch there, "the last seven *hours*, I think it's safe to say that it's not our fucking dog making all that noise."

"There's more than one of them," I said. I moved to the bakery door and turned the key. "Kai might be with them."

"What are you doing?" Terry said. "You think that's wise? I mean, it's not as if you can go out there and *get* him."

I glanced down at the doorknob as my fellow survivors glanced at me. I didn't know what I was doing, but if Kai was out there, being chased by a feral pack, then I wanted to give him easy access. He knew where we were, that the door would be open for him when he returned, and I wasn't going to let him down, not after everything he had done for us.

I eased the door open an inch at a time as the barking got closer and closer; there were so many dogs out there, the noise all seemed to blend into one raucous shout.

"Look!" Jane gasped, her finger poking at the glass. Everyone was at the window now, all except for me. I stood at the door, my heart beating so fast, my head pounding, my fist fucking throbbing from its impact with Dan's stupid mouth.

"There are so *many* of them!" Martha shouted as the dogs raced past the bakery, barking and yapping and howling at the night. The ground was shaking, and the scent of wet dog seemed to filter in to us from the street. "Where are they all *going*?"

I was mesmerised as the sea of dogs flooded along the cobbles outside. There must have been a hundred different breeds there, large and small, long-haired and short. I eased the door shut so that none of them noticed us, but I wanted to call out to Kai, to let him know that if he was there, with *them*, it was safe to come home, but it was far too dangerous. They would tear us apart if they knew we were in here. The only thing hungrier than us were the dogs.

"Looks like they finally gave up on us," Dan said, still dabbing at his mouth with the dusty dishcloth.

Jane began to sob and Terry reached in, wrapped his arms around her to console her.

As the barking dopplered into the distance, I eased the door shut and went to the window. Dan returned to the corner of the room and sat down. Terry took Jane to the kitchen area for a few sips of water – his rations, not hers – as Bob, Martha, and Kelly moved to the counter and covered themselves with sheets.

For almost a full minute waifs and strays galloped by. I stood at the window, watching, and when I saw Kai running alongside a larger terrier, I thought about tapping the glass, to let him know that this was home and we were still here.

I thought about it...

Threepton

NO LEADS?

by Phoebe Cattle.

The local council has stated the increased problem with stray dogs will be dealt with quickly and severely. Councillor Greensmith told the Threepton Observer that any animal found roaming the street will be rounded up and destroyed. The harsh stance from the authorities has not been greeted universally however. Some residents are asking that the dogs should be taken to a shelter and found new home. Councillor Greensmith told this reporter that there are not enough funds to accommodate such a situation at the present time. A member of the opposition party informed us they would resolve the matter more humanely if elected in next Thursday's local elections.

GOOD GIRL

Steven Chapman

Miss Preston smiled as Nicholas Denton mouthed the words of the Threepton Primary School Anthem. The boy bobbed along to the song, opening and closing his mouth like a blissfully ignorant goldfish.

When the song ended, she gathered the children on the brightly coloured play mat for register. Nicholas remained at the far end of the classroom, staring out of the window. The teacher tracked his gormless gaze and caught sight of movement outside.

A dog roamed the playground attempting to decipher the chalk markings on the surface. As it sniffed at the tail of a blue chalk snake wriggling through a ladder, the other children noticed the interloper and abandoned the play mat for a better position at the window.

"Now, now, we've all seen a dog before. I'm sure Mr Buckley will be along soon to help the poor thing get back home"

Lucy Simmons tugged at her teacher's skirt. "I don't like dogs, miss. Make it go away."

Before Miss Preston could respond a second dog appeared.

Lucy began to cry. The teacher scooped up the girl and held her tightly to her chest.

"It's ok, they can't get inside. They're just playing, see? Look, there's Mr Buckley now."

The janitor crossed the playground swinging a short

length of rope at his side. This wasn't the first time a dog had wandered onto the grounds.

Lucy sniffed and snorted, leaving a snail-trail of snot and tears on the shoulder of her teacher's favourite blouse.

Fantastic.

As Mr Buckley reached the animals they bolted, running circles around the old man.

The window began to steam as the children pushed their faces harder against the glass. Miss Preston couldn't help but smirk as Mr Buckley puffed and panted in desperation, trying to catch the trespassers.

A gentle breeze blew papers about as Nicholas opened one of the windows. "Here, doggy!"

"Nicholas, shut that immediately!"

The boy closed the window but remained standing on the sill.

"He'll get in, he'll get in!" Lucy tightened her grip on Miss Preston's neck.

"They can't get in, the window's closed now."

A large collie stopped at the far end of the playground and stared back at the school. Its partner in crime – a Staffordshire bull terrier, all muscle and energy, ready for anything – joined its side.

A third dog burst into view, followed by two more. Miss Preston gaped at the spectacle unfolding before her.

What was happening?

Mr Buckley gave up and sat on a short wall bordering the flowerbeds, tapping numbers into his phone as he caught his breath. Time for reinforcements.

He gave a thumbs-up to the class. Miss Preston shifted the young girl's weight in her arms to return the gesture.

The collie ambled back towards the classroom. The rest of the pack followed.

"They're going to get me," Lucy squealed.

Miss Preston stroked her hair and took a few steps away from the window. "They can't get in. I promise."

The dogs were at the window now.

Miss Preston flinched as she bumped into a table, knocking pens and pencils to the floor.

"Kids, away from the window. Now."

Nicholas fiddled with the window clasps and dangled an arm outside.

Tails wagged.

The dogs exploded.

Meat, muscle, and warm blood spattered against Miss Preston's face. She didn't know whether to burst into hysterics or scream. She looked down to see curves of bone jutting out of Lucy's body. It wasn't clear whether the ribs belonged to the girl or the dogs. It didn't matter, they had done their damage. Blood oozed from ragged holes scattered about Lucy's torso. She was a pin cushion to splintered bone pins.

The damn dogs had just exploded!

A clump of brain matter freed itself from greasy hair and dropped to the floor.

Miss Preston tried to scream as the dead weight of the girl slipped from her arms, but dust clawed down her throat and choked her. Blinking back tears her eyes began to pick out silhouettes of movement cutting through the chaos.

There was no way to recognise which of the children had turned inside out, or which were simply covered in the gore of their classmates.

Mr Buckley clambered through the hole where the window once stood and shouted into his phone for the ambulance to hurry. Miss Preston cradled one of the children in her arms; she couldn't tell which one it was.

Neither of them spotted the other dogs entering the playground.

"Jesus Christ, Kate."

"Hmm?"

Danni prodded her friend. "Are you not watching this?"

Kate Falconer glanced up from her drink to look at the television above the bar. A po-faced reporter stood in the foreground as police and fire crews toiled behind her, slightly out of focus.

"*Witnesses report seeing the dog enter the shopping centre and approach several members of the public before it appeared to choose the victim. It's unclear whether the victim was a target of terrorism, but several eye-witnesses state that the dog exploded...*"

"Did she say 'exploded'?"

"Shhh."

"...more updates as they develop. This is Kelly Randall, reporting for..."

"Jesus, did you hear that? Bloody terrorists using dogs as bombs." Danni took a deep swig from her beer. "So much for your day off."

Kate's eyes remained focused on the television as the feed cut back to the studio. The presenters had moved on to a puff piece, fake smiles lighting up their faces.

This was big. As one of the foremost dog behaviourists in England, Kate had consulted for the police on more than one occasion. They would want to talk to her for sure.

An explosion rumbled in the distance followed by the unmistakable sound of tyres screeching to a halt. A shrill scream and the bar's punters scrambled for the exit. Kate and Danni followed, lunging up the short staircase out onto the street.

A man hurtled past, squeaky brogues slapping against tarmac, tie flapping over his shoulder.

"God damn rubberneckers," Danni said.

Two dogs tore past, panting and tongues lolling as they chased the man. The rest of the crowd headed in the direction of a pillar of smoke rising between two buildings.

The man came to an abrupt halt, gasping for breath. Kate watched the canines flank their target. He dived for an opening but one of the dogs grabbed his ankles pulling him to the floor. It stepped back and resumed a watchful stance. The dogs followed him as he crawled across pavement, maintaining a constant distance from their target.

Kate jumped as the animals exploded. Shards of bone tore the man to pieces. The bloodied remains of one of the dogs' heads rolled to a stop a few metres in front of her, a collar and nametag still attached to the stump that used to be a neck.

Her phone vibrated in her pocket.

❇ ❇ ❇

Kate fidgeted in the rigid chair and drummed her fingers on the table. She gazed at the security camera in the corner of the room and wondered if anyone was watching her. She jumped when the door clicked open. A man entered the room.

"I'm Agent Perkins." He placed a Manila folder on the table and removed his jacket.

"First things first – there are no terrorists."

"What?"

"Everything that's been happening. It's not terrorists; I want to be clear on that" he said, rolling up his shirt sleeves.

"How is that possible? Someone is obviously training these dogs. From what I've seen..."

"Every expert with priority clearance has been working on this for the last 72 hours using the best resources. They cannot find any evidence that the dogs are being manipulated or controlled. They're working independently of humans. That's why we called you in, to figure out why they'd do this."

"Because they've been trained. The dogs I saw, they were working as a team. They were coordinated, following orders."

"As far as we know none of the dogs involved in the incidents so far have had any prior contact. The incident you witnessed this morning – the man killed on Benson Street, outside O'Neill's bar. The Labrador was reported missing over a week ago by a Mrs Cartwright, from Liverpool. And the..." The agent consulted a document in the folder. "the Weimaraner..."

"It's pronounced Vine-maraner."

Perkins raised an eyebrow.

"The Weimaraner," he continued. "broke free from its lead several minutes before the attack."

"They were coordinated. There was blatant communication between the pair, as if they were an established pack."

"I can assure you the dogs had never met before the incident."

"This is preposterous, dogs don't have an agenda, they're not working against us."

"I'd like to believe that, Miss Falconer, but everything we've seen so far tells us otherwise. That's why we called you in, we need someone to help us figure out when and where they're going to attack. So far it seems they're attacking the weak and the wounded, but they're stepping up their game, attacking larger and stronger groups. In the last six hours we've recorded seventeen deaths in Threepton alone."

"I don't know what you want me to do. I can tell you everything you need to know about dog behaviour, but this is unprecedented. I can't predict what they'll do next."

Perkins scooped up his paperwork from the table and tucked it under his arm.

"This might be easier to explain if we go to the lab."

He left the room and Kate followed.

"The attacks have increased exponentially over the past twelve hours. What the news has reported is only a fraction of incidents. We need to find them and end this now."

The pair reached a door at the end of the corridor. Perkins stopped.

"What I'm about to show you is top secret. If you can't help we need to know now and we need to know fast."

Kate nodded "I'll advise you as best I can."

Perkins opened the door. The room was huge but there was barely space to manoeuvre, with equipment taking up most of the available floor area. White lab coats fretted from machine to machine. Several dogs lay strapped to hospital gurneys with doctors monitoring even more equipment.

"It's a little bit more complicated than that, Miss Falconer."

"Daddy, no!"

Tim ignored his children's pleas.

He barked out for his wife to hold the children back as he pulled Colin out of the back door.

"And keep them the hell inside, whatever you hear."

The door slammed behind him as he dragged the mutt

by the collar to the back of the garden. The shed door resisted. He slapped the wall once the door was open, searching for the light switch. The weak bulb flickered to life, barely illuminating the workspace. Still, it was enough for the task at hand. With the door bolted from the inside, he let go of the collar.

Colin circled the shed sniffing at tools, plant pots and everything else at nose level.

Tim sat on an old padded chair and sighed.

"Fuck."

Colin snapped his head round to his master. The dog plodded over to Tim and sat in front of him, his head turned to the side as if waiting instruction.

"I'm sorry, little buddy, I really am."

Tim picked up a spade that was leaning against the potting bench and turned it around and around in his hands.

"But if I don't do it, they will soon enough."

The emergency broadcast aired before the Ten o'clock News last night. It had urged all households to 'dispose' of their dogs. *Jesus, what a shitty way to phrase it.* Dispose – such diplomacy, and yet every dog owner in Threepton knew what it meant. It meant kill your dog. Commit murder on man's best friend.

Colin had been part of the family for seven years and Tim would be damned if he'd let them take him. But he had seen the footage, the children lying dead in playgrounds, the unforgettable scenes of streets full of mutilated corpses, impossible to tell dog carcass from human. He was doing the right thing by his family, but it was of little comfort in the cold, musty confines of the shed. If he let the government take Colin, they'd stick him in the back of a truck full of strange dogs, take him somewhere desolate, and put him down without an ounce of compassion. The old mutt deserved better. He was a good dog. The best.

Tim put the shovel to the side for a moment and leant in to hold his dog. He wrapped his arms around the fluffy mess of fur and squeezed. Colin wagged, his whole body wobbled from side to side. He twisted his head around so he could lick his master's face, and his master let him. Colin licked and licked, and wagged with all his might. He bounced, unable to contain the excitement in a stationary body.

Tim stood and Colin turned in a circle, knocking a pot off a shelf with his tail. He investigated the mess behind him and, sheepishly, looked up to his master.

"It's ok, Colin, you did nothing wrong. You're a good boy."

Tim picked up the shovel again and wrung his hands around the shaft. He raised the tool as high as he could in the low confines of the shed.

"You're a good boy."

The last thing Daisy saw of Tim, was his bloody carcass flying out of the shed window.

She screamed for her husband.

The children screamed for Colin.

�֍ ✖ ✖

"You want to put my brain in a dog's body?"

"Your consciousness, Miss Falconer, not your physical brain. The procedure is completely reversible."

"You make it sound so simple, as if I'm popping in to have my appendix removed. Level with me, how safe can it really be?"

"I understand your trepidation, but we wouldn't go ahead with the procedure if it wasn't completely safe. You're our best chance at finding out what the dogs are going to do next. We need an answer…"

"Fast – I know, but this is quite a lot to take in, you know? I'm sorry I'm not strapping myself into Dr Frankenstein's workbench and chomping at the bit to get going."

"The process is a little more delicate than that, I can assure you. This is something we've been working with for a long time. Not only is it completely safe, it's quite liberating."

"You've done it?"

"Several times. I wouldn't expect any of my staff to do something I wouldn't do myself."

"No shit."

"The process is the easy part – the hard part will be fitting in with the pack."

"So let me get this straight, you want me to upload my brain into an comatose animal, infiltrate a pack of detonating dogs terrorising the country, all the while not letting on that I am in fact not a dog, but a civilian wearing a damn convincing canine suit?"

"We need to know where the main groups are concentrated so we can take care of them as quickly as possible."

"You mean kill them?"

"You have another suggestion?"

"It's not their fault."

"Yesterday, an operations team in Leeds tried to round up some of the canine subjects to see if they could be 'disarmed'. As soon as they began transporting the dogs, they all exploded. Every single member of the team is dead. The force of the explosion was so great it ripped a hole in the road the size of a small car. It may not be their fault, Miss Falconer, but there's little else we can do at this point."

Calm down, Kate. Calm down.

"Lie back and try not to worry."

Kate raised an eyebrow at the technician as she leaned back into the soft cushion of the gurney. She looked over at the dog resting on another table at the back of the room.

The technician spoke softly, with a fondness in his voice. "She's a bitch – doesn't have a name, she was raised in the lab. All of the dogs we send in are bitches actually. It makes the transference process a little easier."

Kate looked away from the dog, feeling guilty about using it in such an invasive manner.

A yellow legal pad page had been taped to the ceiling above her – 'Scientists do it doggy style!' filled the paper in large scrawled letters.

The technician smiled "Lab humour. Now close your eyes, please, Miss Falconer."

He placed tape over Kate's eyelids. The urge to open them was almost unbearable.

"This won't take long. Deep breaths please, and relax, we need to slow your heart rate down."

Kate concentrated on her breathing. She counted off each lungful of air and focused on the numbers.

An odd sensation crept through her body before erupting into static numbness. It felt as if she were being yanked backwards by a large hand tugging at her spine. She tried to take a deep breath but there was no air. Opening her mouth to cry out for help proved impossible, her jaw didn't want to cooperate. There was a looseness to it and it suddenly lolled and drooped as if it was broken. Kate concentrated and finally took a breath. She opened her eyes and looked around the room.

Her whole body twitched with anticipation. There was a subtlety to the muscles now, a lightness. But there was also power behind them, a kind of restfulness. As if they weren't happy being stationary and she needed to run and sprint through grass and woodland. The urge to move forward was unbearable. Kate wriggled from side to side on the table. Then she saw it, out of the corner of her new eyes – a hairy length of black fur swooping back and forth. It was mesmerising. Something in the movement excited her in a way she had never experienced before.

She felt hands on her side and looked over to see the technician pressing a stethoscope against her chest. The metal wasn't as cold as she expected, and she realised it was her new fur coat protecting her from the shocking chill of the equipment.

A new sensation crept through her canine body. A feeling of warmth and happiness. She rested her head back on the table and closed her eyes. Her body thrummed as her tail smacked the table over and over.

"Kate, I need to ask you a few questions and you're going to have to try your hardest to respond. I need you to move your front right leg if you understand me."

Kate thought about the request, half tempted to ignore it and remain in a state of restfulness. But she had a job to do, lives were at stake. She concentrated on the gangly legs before her. They looked so peculiar from her angle. The right leg twitched. *Not the leg, my leg. You can do this, Kate. Move your damn leg.*

She shoved the leg forward, her claws sliding across the metal surface.

"I'll take that as a yes," the technician said, making a note on his tablet.

"Now we need to try and get you mobile. I'm going to untie the straps and then I want you to try and roll over for me."

Kate tried to laugh at the request, but it came out as a cross between a choked cough and a failed hiccup. Her head tilted to the side in response to the sound.

She glanced over to see herself laid out on a gurney. Her body was hooked up to equipment that kept her breathing and her heart beating.

The technician saw where Kate was looking. "We'll keep you nice and safe while you're gone."

It took a few minutes of skittering and scrabbling but Kate made it to her new feet. Standing on four legs rather than two was an odd feeling, but she adapted quicker than she'd anticipated.

"Take it nice and slow to start with. It's going to take a while to get accustomed to your new anatomy. We know some form of muscle memory is retained by the body during transference. Now, let's try a few of the basics."

The technician made Kate perform a series of simple tasks – walking to certain points in the room and turning around, a slight gallop when she was more confident, and even a test bark to get used to her new voice.

"Good girl," the technician praised.

Kate growled.

The technician smirked, "Sorry, force of habit, but it's good to hear you can do that. You may need it."

Kate watched the soldiers climb into the van, each carrying an impressive array of weapons. A strong coppery smell filled her nose and she sniffed at one of the soldiers as he walked past. Was it the guns that smelled so pungent?

The technician snapped his fingers to get Kate's attention. He pointed at an oversized keypad next to the external door and over-exaggerated pressing the numbers once again for her benefit.

"One-eight-one-two, see? The 1812 Overture. The one with the cannons, easy to remember. Whatever you do, don't forget it. The soldiers round here are a little edgy so no hanging around. You'll want to tap in the code as quickly as possible and then we'll know it's you. And it should go without saying but don't bring any other dogs back with you."

The closer the car got to the drop off point, the more excited Kate became. She knew she should be frightened, but all the tension and the stress seemed to be seeping out of her in a tingling sensation that vibrated her whole body. Her borrowed body. She could feel her tail moving, but it was trapped between her and the car seat. Unable to wag the energy was transferred into a bum and shoulder wiggle that made it look like she was dancing away to a song only she could hear.

The car screeched to a stop and Kate found herself in the footwell of the vehicle. Legs pumped and scrabbled but it was no good, she was trapped face down in the dark space. Oh god, how am I going to get...what's that smell? With nostrils flared, the odour seemed to grow stronger. It was food, of that she was sure, but what kind? Was there any left? Could she find?

A cool breeze tickled her fur and she felt hands on her flanks. Someone was pulling her out of the car. She tried to get one last noseful of stink before she left the vehicle.

"We're as near as we can get without them seeing us. They seem to be concentrated in this area. Head north for about half a mile and you should start seeing them. After that it's up to you."

Kate wagged at the technician. She cocked her head to the side and studied him. The man was pointing to the side.

"North. Half a mile. You understand?"

Kate attempted to nod but instead her head wobbled about as if it had come loose. She barked instead to show her understanding.

He recoiled.

"Jesus, you wanna keep it down? Get out of here before they see us together."

He jumped in the car and peeled away from the kerb in a plume of smoke and exhaust fumes.

Kate didn't need to sniff at the air; the stink permeated every fibre of her being. She sneezed and the world tumbled in all directions at once. A quick sniff at where the car had been. She set off north.

The streets were empty. With the public on mass alert and a curfew in effect, she doubted she would see anyone. She could smell them though. There were traces of people everywhere. Their scents overwhelmed her. It was like being in a noisy pub and trying to pick out a single conversation.

Something had urinated on the base of a nearby

lamppost. It smelt as if she'd wandered into public toilets that had never been cleaned. She tried to wrinkle her nose in disgust but it didn't translate into her dog muscles. *Why the hell did dogs go nuts for that smell?* It was worse for them than it was for humans.

She padded over to the other side of the street. Food had been dropped there recently. It smelt like chips, another sniff, and some kind of meat. It smelt delicious.

A dog barked in the distance and her ears sprang to attention. *Remember why you're here Kate.* She walked in the direction of the sound, accelerating into a trot and then a gallop, relishing the new sensation on her feet. As she turned the corner she came face to face with a pack of dogs. Three of them – a German Shepherd, a Greyhound, and a Border Collie – standing to attention as if waiting for her. She admonished herself. Of course, they were waiting for her; they were more accustomed to picking out individual scents from the plethora of odours currently assaulting their noses. Kate concentrated and tried to pick out the scents of the dogs, but it was hard to tell which was which.

The hounds advanced without any of the usual excitable tension that dogs exhibit when meeting for the first time. The German Shepherd approached and Kate tried to stand as still as possible. Dogs couldn't actually smell fear, but they were better than even the most accomplished human psychologist at recognising it in behaviour. Kate looked at the dogs but didn't force eye contact, worrying that her stares might be misinterpreted as an act of aggression. But if she looked away too much, the dogs could see her as an easy target.

The Greyhound walked in long leisurely strides and circled behind Kate. She remained facing the leader of the pack. She could feel the dog behind her, and she could hear it sniffing. *Perfectly normal behaviour.* The dogs were checking her out, assessing whether she was a threat or not. This was a good sign. If the dogs had reason to be cautious of each other then it might mean they hadn't all turned.

Kate waited a moment before deciding to be bold. She approached the dogs, using her nose to familiarise herself with her new canine friends. The smells were new but somehow recognisable. Longstride, the dog that had sniffed her from behind was young and male. The Border Collie was male and stank of shit and filth. Whatever he had rolled in had been rotten as sin. The smile on his face told Kate that Shitstink was pleased as punch with the smell.

The leader, also male, was old, with a grey beard and...Kate closed her eyes and scented again. He was ill. Dying. She felt a twinge of empathy and also respect. The dog was facing the end with dignity, carrying on its normal duties and looking after its own. Whatever the reason for the dogs' actions, they were sticking together. No race wars, or religion to argue about. It was them versus humans. Versus *us!* Us. A dog's body, but still human.

Be careful, Kate. Be careful.

※ ※ ※

Threepton was deserted, the residents barricaded in their homes. The pack padded down the road with Kate at the back. They were moving fast and Kate had to break into a canter to keep up. More dogs joined them along the route. So far, all the dogs she encountered had been male. According to Agent Perkins, bitches hadn't been involved in any of the incidents so far. Kate wasn't sure what to make of that fact.

The ground was warm underpaw, still heated from soaking up the sun's rays during the day. Everything felt new and different, each sensation making her beam with happiness. As the group picked up speed she felt as if her whole body was smiling, a tingling sensation that lifted her to a different place. The faster they ran, the faster she wanted to go. They were free and heading somewhere and the single-mindedness of it was tremendous. Her tongue lolled and she took delight in the wind rushing across her face and fur.

Greybeard veered right and the group darted into an alley lined with cardboard boxes and overflowing dustbins. They moved like a flock of birds, in one fluid movement, as one mind.

At the end of the alley the dogs leapt a fence. There was no time to slow down, instinct took over. Legs pumped, Kate coiled down at the last moment and pushed hard with her back legs. She felt invincible as she cleared the top of the fence and landed softly on the other side.

The pack was waiting for her. Greybeard sniffed at her flanks and nudged her with his nose. She was too caught up in the moment to realise what he was doing. The dog mounted her, his paws flailing at her sides in an attempt to balance himself. She slumped under the weight of the larger dog as her front legs gave way. She was lying in prone position and the dog took it as a sign of submission.

Kate panicked and dropped her back legs so she fell flat to the floor. The older dog didn't react quickly enough and the abrupt drop caused him to yelp. He rolled to the side and lay in the dust panting and confused.

Kate rose to her paws and turned to face the old dog. She let out a fierce growl. The German Shepherd was too tired to retaliate, he laid still and attempted to catch his breath before standing. Kate felt a nip of guilt. The old boy was only following instinct...but it wasn't her world, and she had to keep some kind of separation.

The pack continued onwards, they didn't have to travel much further before they reached their destination. Longstride slipped between two bushes growing against a wall and disappeared. Kate watched as Shitstink and the other dogs followed suit, Greybeard casting a glance in her direction before he too disappeared into the void.

Kate looked around and marvelled at the dogs' understanding of tactics. Not only was the entrance cleverly masked, there was nowhere in the surrounding area from where it could be seen. The only way to know it was there was to follow the dogs down the alley, and Kate could only assume they were too smart to allow themselves to be tailed.

Leaves dragged across her snout as she shuffled through the foliage. She squinted hard to avoid the thorns striking her eyes. When she opened them she found herself in a dark abyss. The smell of other dogs was intoxicating. Kate followed her nose, taking bold steps into the darkness. The further she went the more she could smell and hear. There were mewls and growls and barks from deep inside the building.

Her canine eyes grew accustomed to the gloom. She was in a corridor.

Concrete turned to metal as she found herself on a platform high above a factory floor. The dogs numbered in the thousands, and Kate could feel her hackles raise as she realised one mistake would be the end of her mission. Maybe her life.

But she had found it, and it had been easier than she could have ever expected. Now it was time to get the hell out of here and get back to the lab. She turned back and bumped noses with Greybeard.

She tried to step around him but he mirrored her movements. As Kate snarled three large dogs appeared from the platform and took their place next to the German Shepherd.

She was trapped.

Trent stopped. He glanced at the wheelie bin to his right. *Nope, I'm ok.* He carried on, then spun on his heels and threw open the lid to the bin, purging the contents of his stomach into it, some missing the receptacle and hitting the floor. Wiping his mouth on the back of his jacket sleeve he laughed as he noticed he had vomited into a recycling bin.

Trent jumped as something nudged him from behind. He had to grab hold of the bin to stop himself from toppling over. A small Staffordshire terrier was nuzzling at the back of his legs and he moved out of its way, skirting around the bin, keeping hold of the plastic lip. The dog dived for the pool of warm vomit and began to lap at the puddle.

"Oh, Christ. You dirty little bastard."

Trent kicked out, but the dog easily dodged the drunken attack and went immediately back to its meal.

"You think I'm scared of you, mate. You haven't met my wife."

He snorted at his own remark and weaved down the path to the end of his street. Something tickled the back of his legs and he turned to see the Staffie staring up at him, licking its lips.

"Fuck off," Trent said, the boozy confidence fading.

The dog responded by sitting down.

"Good dog...now stay."

Trent backed away and the dog stayed put.

He increased his pace. He could see his house from here, the living room light glowing in the darkness of the street. Oh, shit – Rita's still up. *No getting out of this one, time to take your punishment like a man.*

The world tumbled as the pavement rose to meet his face. The damn dog was yanking at his trouser legs, even as he lay on the floor shouting in agony.

"Get the fuck off me," he yelled, the fear cutting through his booze-addled stupor.

His foot connected with the dog and it yelped as it landed a few feet away.

"Little shit."

Trent scrambled forward and pulled himself to his feet with the help of a neighbour's garden wall. He turned and saw the dog lying motionless just beyond the kerb. A sigh of relief turned into a laugh. He rubbed his face. *Jesus, dealing with Rita is going to be a piece of piss now.*

He peered over the tops of his hands and saw the Doberman standing in front of him. Another Doberman nudged at the motionless Staffie, before joining the other dog's side.

The Dobermans growled.

Trent screamed.

✖ ✖ ✖

The pack led Kate down a staircase into the main throng of canines. Dogs mingled on the factory floor, sitting or standing in smaller groups. There was no segregation between the canines – large dogs mixed with small, different breeds walked with each other. None of them paid attention to Kate.

She could hear her own claws tapping in the silence. An occasional bark or whimper were the only things to break the calm. Kate stopped to scan the crowd. The dogs weren't rabid or diseased, they were disciplined. They were organised.

Greybeard nudged her from behind and Kate lurched forward.

As they reached the back of the room, an archway opened into a maze of hallways. There was a musky scent in the air and Kate's nose twitched as she tried to identify the odour. The dogs at the front of the pack grew excited as the smell grew stronger.

Kate recognised the scent as they turned the last corner and saw them. It was the musky odour of a bitch in heat. Hundreds in fact. Dogs groped at the bitches as they mated in eerie silence.

The guard dogs either side of Kate began to yip and chuff in excitement, but remained by her side.

They'd brought her here to reproduce. That was why she hadn't seen any bitches along the way; they were being used to breed an army. Kate did the maths in her head. If the dogs remained hidden and bred at a standard rate they could replenish ranks faster than the military could cope. *God knows how many more places like this exist.*

Then another thought dawned on her. All the agents they had sent in so far had been transformed into bitches. That meant they could be here right now. Trapped by the other dogs, forced into sexual labour. Kate felt sick. She needed to get out of here and warn Perkins.

The dogs blocked her exit, and already males were sniffing around her in hopes of fucking. She couldn't let them take her.

She lunged for the nearest dog and head butted him in the side, using her momentum to push him over the edge of the high platform.

The dog hit the concrete floor with a crunch, dead instantly. She turned to the other pursuers and growled. She bared teeth and snapped at another dog's neck. Teeth sank into flesh and Kate shook her head from side to side. The dog yelped but she ignored the pleas and finished her gruesome task.

Blood seeped down her gullet, she couldn't spit it out. Instead she swallowed the metallic tasting fluid and turned to the dogs that had led her into the room.

They hesitated. Kate grabbed Greybeard by the back leg and bit down hard. The old dog yelped and tried to pull away but the harder he pulled the harder she clamped down. The German Shepherd collapsed to the floor howling in pain.

Another guard dog jumped onto Kate's back and gripped onto her neck with a powerful bite. She lay on the floor assuming a submissive state. Her attacker relinquished his grip ever so slightly. It was enough. She jerked her head to the side, freeing herself, and leapt back onto all fours. She barked as loud as she could, spittle flying from her muzzle.

One last push should do it. Kate looked down at Greybeard wishing she could explain why she had to do this. She grabbed a hold of the Shepherd's neck and with one violent twist, snapped the old boy's neck.

She bared her blood-soaked teeth and took a single step toward the remaining dogs. They backed away, their heads lowered.

Kate turned to look out over the factory floor, her breath coming in ragged gasps.

One by one the dogs began to howl into the void above them. Their cries built to a crescendo that cut through Kate's fury and calmed her.

She joined them.

✖ ✖ ✖

The pack ran. Kate led the dogs through woodland, galloping past great oak trunks spiking from the ground, paws hammering against sodden earth. The odours from the soil and rotting leaves were peaceful and familiar. This was where she belonged, her heart finally beating with a purpose. She could feel each sinewy muscle pumping and contracting, leading her closer to her target. She was born for this and this alone.

Up ahead there were lights. The woods were ending. Sadness filled her heart. She turned back to face the trees and saw the pack, her pack, waiting, panting, eager. Ready to take orders.

The streets were still deserted, though the military could be waiting around any corner. It was time for stealth. No more running, claws skittering against stone. Her pack followed her on silent paws. Into the city.

✖ ✖ ✖

Alex Mathers watched the monitors with half shut eyes. Blinks became longer and longer until she began to dream. Slipping off the chair jolted her back into the land of the living and she made a point of standing up to stop herself from dropping off again. She slapped both cheeks, tapping out a staccato rhythm on fleshy jowls.

"Stay awake, stay awake."

A deep sniff followed by a heavy sigh. Alex reached for her cup but found it empty. The coffee pot under the desk was currently burning something that resembled tar from a smoker's lung. She grabbed the pot and took it into a small room behind the reception desk. With a fresh pot of coffee on the boil she dashed to the toilets located behind the lifts. No one would miss her for two minutes, it had been a quiet night anyway.

As her bladder emptied, Alex rubbed her eyes and groaned. She checked her watch. Only another two hours to go and then you can sleep all bloody weekend. Two measly hours.

Back at her station she poured herself a cup. Five sugars later she took a sip and sighed. The time would fly by.

Movement in the corner of her eye. She turned. The monitors were showing the same views of the inside and outside of the building. Nothing unusual on screen, but something had caught her attention. There! Monitor number two, a flash of black zoomed from one end of the screen to the other. Then another flash, lighter this time. Alex grabbed the control keyboard and hit full screen. With the other hand, she manoeuvred the joystick and panned camera two to the right.

The dogs were gathering against the south wall of the yard. Alex steered the camera around, switching between the few cameras that overlooked the yard.

She squinted at the screen.

One of the dogs was staring at the door, doing something with the...

Oh god.

Alex ran.

Numbers. The way in. Numbers open door.

Kate struggled to remember the combination. Stopping was almost painful. She needed to be moving forward, doing something, but she persisted, front paws on the wall, keypad at eye level.

Numbers.

She could hear music in her head, a familiar tune. Something she had listened to many times before. It was the key to the numbers.

Wet nose touched metal and she jumped when the pad beeped in response.

One. *That was it!*

Eight. *It was definitely eight.* She fell into the song playing inside her mind. *The cannons!* She could hear the cannons.

One. *It was so obvious.*

Two.

The keypad beeped three times and the door popped open an inch. Kate pushed her nose inside the gap, forcing it wider. With her head wedged in the gap the heavy door opened easily. She was almost inside when she spotted the woman.

The human slammed her weight against the door and Kate yelped in pain as she heard ribs crack. She felt her pack sniffing at her from behind as they investigated her calls. They pushed and clawed at the door and Kate howled as she was shoved from both sides.

More and more dogs crowded around Kate and the pressure against her side subsided. She howled again, calling her pack into action and the woman cried out in anguish as the dogs applied more weight to the entrance. Slowly the door opened enough for Kate to slip inside. A growl forced the woman back a few paces, but she was a brave one this human and she didn't run when she had the chance. The woman removed a radio from her belt and spoke into it.

Kate stopped and tilted her head.

She understood the words but they were fuzzy, as if she was remembering them from a dream. She continued onwards, slowly approaching the human.

The woman's hand dipped into a pocket and pulled out a cylinder the size of a torch. She pressed a trigger on top of the device and Kate shrunk into the floor as an ultrasonic burst of noise filled the corridor. The rest of the pack fled back into the outside world.

The woman stepped forward, confident with her weapon, and forced Kate back towards the entrance.

It can't hurt. It's just noise.

Kate tried to force her body forward, to ignore the sound, but it refused. Some part of her was terrified by the sound.

Kate's tail brushed the door, she was running out of

room, but the woman would have to step around her to close it. As the woman's gaze darted towards the door and Kate seized the advantage, launching herself from the floor, mouth open wide ready to sink her teeth into the human's neck. As the handheld device dropped to the floor, the shrill sound of the ultrasonic repellent dissolved into the woman's piercing screams. It wasn't long before the screams turned to gurgles. The pack returned to watch.

Kate could feel the young woman's blood washing down her throat. It was still warm and tasted exquisite. It filled her with life and she refused to let go. She shook from side to side, her scissor grip tearing chunks of flesh from the woman's neck.

The pack watched eagerly as Kate finished off her first human.

✵ ✵ ✵

More guards poured into the room. The ones that could comprehend the carnage without freezing in fear managed a few kills. Mostly dogs that were otherwise occupied ripping the throats from their colleagues. The dogs paying attention to the guards exploded with enough force to rock the building on its foundations. The humans never stood a chance.

Kate led her charges from room to room, killing any living creature they found. When they reached the experimentation chamber, the dogs began to howl in unison at the site of their fallen comrades. Three scientists cowered in the corner, shivering behind ruined machines and covered in the gore of their lab partners. Kate breathed in their fear then finished them off with her fellow canines.

There was one last room to visit. Kate went alone. She tugged at the sleeve of the hospital gown until the body fell from the gurney to the floor. She looked herself in the eye, but it wasn't her anymore – it was a stranger. It was the enemy. Kate bit into the neck of the body she used to inhabit and waited until the pulse slowed, then stopped altogether.

With the transformation equipment destroyed, and the scientists responsible dead, there was no way for the humans to find her pack. They were free. She felt a warm tingle spreading throughout her body – a flame setting her soul on fire.

She had done her job. She was happy. She was good.

Good girl, Kate. Good girl.

PAST LIVES.

Were you Cleopatra in another life? Once Marilyn Monroe? Do you dream of other times before you were born? Do you have memories of being Napoleon, or even Churchill? Whatever your future holds the past may be the key.

Past life regression and hypnosis. Call local number to book. Cash payments only. No cheques from your former self.

Call Richard Baron on 07465

QUEEN BITCH

Lily Childs

The Queen is dead. Long live...freedom.

The land is as barren as her late majesty; her subjects as blind. We worked long and hard to maintain a state of misery on the monarch's behalf but whilst we are now free, the memory of her reigns over us still. Queen Sophie Russell; an obese, violent bitch. I picture her in her final days, a squat toad of a dog lying on a once-vermillion cushion, eyes silver with cataracts as she roars out orders. Her drool is venomous, for with it comes years of infection, spraying from that stinking hole of a mouth. She is all incisors, the other teeth dead and decayed – but incisors are all she needs. Her slaves, Tom and Irene Boakes, are scarred in skin and soul. Even to feed the beast meant taking their lives into their own hands. But rejoice! For today, gross belly undulating from the heat of her overworked heart, the self-proclaimed queen stopped breathing.

My brothers whine and piss themselves when the key is brought. Their fear is understandable – but no longer warranted.

"She's dead," I whisper. They don't hear me.

Every day for however long it was, each of us was given 'play time' with Sophie – for Sophie's benefit. The Boakes were under the illusion all their cherub needed was to be with her own kind, to feel canine compassion. We were left in the small enclave, barely bigger than a box, for Sophie to lash out words of derision and spite, to attack what she could not see – frequently wounding my brothers. How any living being could justify the assault of one upon another defies comprehension, but she had the Boakes under her spell. She put the idea in their heads, caused them too to be blind – as blind as new-born pups; blind to what was right.

But a queen is a queen is a queen. Queen Bitch is dead. Long live her successor.

C'est moi, mon cher.

I'd have eaten her myself if I could. The size of me, the wile of me suggests the appropriate power. I've been biding my time, t'is all. Her subjects despised yet feared to deride her – all the better to take control once the demon departed. I am ready. But energies such as Sophie Russell do not leave easily. Humans talk of ghosts, and of spirits and poltergeists. They trouble themselves with science and the neverness of death, relating it all to themselves, as humankind. But life is older than them, death older still. Revival, reincarnation... let me tell you something. YOU were a dog once; a foul-smelling ravenous hunter. Skin barely hung from your bones, blood barely stuck to your teeth before you licked it away and ran in search of your next prey – for pleasure or gain.

Ball-busting humans with their fancy talk and their upright walk; they're the evangelists of evolution – *look at me; all modern and new and knowing it all.* Choose a thousand new-agers (if you really must; the thought makes my gut hurt). They will tell you they're the reincarnation of Cleopatra or Marilyn Monroe, that their totem animal is the eagle, the coyote or the wild, wild wolf. Let's face the facts; there's not enough of that shit to go around. And if you think Chief Sitting Bull's sitting on your left shoulder? You're deluded. Hopelessly. Sitting Bull done sitting way back in his own lifetime. Shitting on you, more like – 'cause you're all fools.

Twenty Betty ready, ain't no hound dog, hound dog
Freakin' out the masters with her... smile
Making plans each day just like it's ground hog, ground hog
Summoning the strength to vamp her style.

I killed the Boakes last night. With my teeth. Showed those brothers of mine how it's done, fucking cowards.

You sneak, see. All eyes and cuteness; that hang-dog expression learned from years of subjugation – well, some of us. And there's you thinking, how does a Jack Russell look cute in any way, shape or form? Did I *tell* you I was a terrier? When did I ever mention my brothers were rabbit-busting bastards with nothing between their ears to tell them when to stop? Fuck no – it's worse than that.

We're adorable.

We're spaniels.

Big eyes, long ears, long hair and a propensity for

affection. We don't do bad. Sometimes though, things have to change.

Your concern for the Boakes, if you have any respect for them at all, will surely diminish twelve-fold at the idea they could place a heaving genocidal maniac in charge of a litter of loping, friendly pups. This is assuming you're regarding the concept from a human perspective. Is it too much for you to consider the situation may have been contrived by Ms Bitch herself? (Note the 'Ms' – a life less loved by another canine could barely be possible.) It is my understanding she, over many years, influenced the Boakes to take on a petite smallholding; large enough to provide kennels for breeding dogs, small enough to appear homely. Irene claimed the business was her idea; Tom likewise and they would argue with enough embarrassing banter to turn their few friends against them until no one ventured past their door aside from fee-paying clients who believed the lies to suit them. Sophie Bannatista Glorimund Up-Your-Fucking Arsehole Russell was nothing more than a groomer; a contriver. My guess is she'd been around for a long time before Irene rescued her and had been abusing dogs and humans since she fell from her mother's womb.

Had I the right to hold court, I would have done so years ago. Men and women, they shove their criminals before judge and jury with who knows what kind of propensities. I've seen the corvids do it too – crows, maggot-pies and jackdaws casting judgement on wayward teenagers or alien species. There is much to respect in these parliaments yet every difference between a raven decision and a human one. A rook and his courtly brethren will think nothing of banishing a wrong-doer. They take longer to ponder an execution but when the decision is made, the result is cruel and public.

Well, who am I to judge? A docile, cream and tan mutt with a love of life and eyes to melt into? I tell you this. I have everything to judge. I watched my six brothers tremble and defecate themselves into an existence of pure terror whilst the Boakes clapped and worshipped at the filthy feet of Queen Russell. Two died within as many months of weaning, our mother ripped from their hungry mouths and sent on to another kennel for more fucking and childbirth, poor bitch. Our father, regal in his own way, developed renal dysfunction and struggled for weeks in agony until Tom 'had him removed.'

Things will be different around here from now on. We're going to learn how to hunt. Flush stupid birds out from the undergrowth but catch them for ourselves, not for some twat with a gun who would ram the thing full of shot then spit pellets onto his plate.

My brothers come crawling towards me, back legs all-a-quiver, tails so low you'd think them docked.

"Come lads," I say. "You don't want to be afraid of me. I'm going to show you a better life."

Rollo raises his head. "Betty – we liked it the way it was."

The four of them are up and out the door in fear of my retribution. They must have seen it in my eyes. Idiots. Why humans want to breed these dumb-ass canines is a mystery to me.

☓ ☓ ☓

Alone.

Bored, pocked and alone.

Rollo, Sheldon, Leibnitz and Kurtz – they didn't follow me after all. I ran so far, so fast, expecting them to follow my trail, inspired by my strength and resolve. They are dead to me; just like Sophie, like the Boakes and my father. I always felt I was superior – now I know it for sure.

Run.

Run.

Run.

Run.

The hole in my right leg is suppurating. Who'd have thought the wild was so… wild. I'd tripped over something metal, something *barbed* not two days hence. Flies gather the slower I run. It's not just the leg; I'd coursed through a barrier of giant hemlock and now my face is losing skin. There is bone where once there was fur. My right nostril is twice the size of the left and drips incessantly. I fear my eyes will be next to go in which case Sophie will have won, even in death.

It's cold. Never would I have expected such tremors, such shuddering. I hear whining and want to shriek at the weak creature in my midst but I kind of know it is me and the voice that slides from my throat confirms my hypothesis. I fall to the wet grass; darkness is falling too but the moon is high. The combination is the worst for my night vision. Vague images blend together, confusing the forests and the skies. I've lost my primal reactions. It should be easier than this.

Sirens scream in the distance; they've discovered the Boakes. Maybe I'll head to the coast and search out the sirens there, the sea-kind. The type that will lure me to their bosom with a death serenade then reveal themselves, teeth as sharp as mine, claws for the killing. I pull myself up as best I can, back legs dragging like an old mongrel ready for the needle. The dream draws me on, the imagined briny scent prickling my diseased nasal passages.

> *I'm pining for your wave,*
> *A salty sea-dog, me*
> *The lap of your embrace*
> *Your wetness on my face.*
> *A salty sea-dog, me.*
> *A salty sea-dog.*
> *Me.*

It's as though I remember a time, before all this... before the Boakes and the Bitch, the brothers and sick, sick, sick reality of the present day. Who ruled then, I wonder. And what was I? Here I am now, getting caught in that New Age trap of reincarnation I was so careful to dispute but it all seems so real. Me, on a galley, bare feet running all around me, the occasional hand reaching out to rub my ear. Calm waters. Storms. Wreckage. Drowning... I drowned, that was it! If I can only find the place I washed up I'll be able to save my soul; redeem my tragic death.

Run.
Run.
Run.
Not so much running.
Walking now.
Tripping.
A little lie-down, that'll do the job.

"Who do you think she belongs to?"

There are voices in my head.

"Do you think she's chipped?"

They're not my voice. Blood seeps into my eye as I crack the scab open to look out. I'm on a boat. I've gone back in time to the olden days.

"We ought to get her to a vet; they'll know what to do. Poor thing."

I'm not convinced. Modern things like electricals, devices and a TV are squashed into the small galley. I'm no canine pirate Queen. I'm a near-dead bitch on a crappy old barge with a pair of do-gooders trying to work out how to save my life. How the fuck did I get here?

Glorious mud, they call it. I'm in touch with that. Nothing like a roll in the black stuff, but by the stink that suddenly hits me, I reckon I must have taken a nosedive straight into a mire of river sludge. I squeeze the other eye open to check myself out. An involuntary yelp, all high-pitched and girly, erupts from my throat. I growl in spite of myself. Looking down, it's almost as if I'm not here; at the most, a murk-laden shadow. There is no cream, there is no tan, just hair completely coated in filth.

An attractive couple are peering at me. She too has mud at the ends of her long golden tresses; he has no shirt on but his arms are covered in a sticky mess up to the elbows. Well, thank you for the lift guys, but I'd best be going. You don't want to be seen hanging out with a criminal. You'll go down for it.

Naked boy reaches for a phone.

Naked boy no longer has a phone, nor does he have a hand with which to finger numbers on a screen, or worse. I match his screaming with a howl whilst his little dolly girlfriend cowers in the corner and he attempts to batter me with some soft weapon he's grabbed with his remaining hand.

"Fucking. Bitch." He can't articulate between sobs.

"Why yes, yes I am. I'm the new Queen Bitch, haven't you heard?"

They don't understand me so I scarper up short wooden steps, out onto the deck (nothing like in my day) and take a leap.

The tide must have come in while I was taking that nap. Fast-flowing, it is. Seaweed gets caught around my legs as I struggle to swim and I shift between the pleasure of being washed clean and the fear of drowning… again.

Has it really come to that?

I give in and let the flow take me as far it wants, which turns out to be not that far at all. I'm meandering down a tributary, half-paddling, half-walking. My head's above the water, now my flanks, now my feet until I'm tottering on rocks like a slut on vodka. That's what Irene used to drink before I killed her. She liked her "'ickle tot of voddie please, Tom?" every ten minutes, whilst Tom could neck a litre of whisky a night without even passing out. Pissheads. The night I tore their throats out I almost expected their blood to ignite.

There's a small cove ahead below an embankment. Shingle creeps between my toes, sand sticks to my torn pads but I limp across the beach onto grass and hope if I can just rest again for the tiniest of moments that no one will come and get me. That no one will put me down.

Rabbits.

Rabbits and bony birds, plants that make me vomit, water that gives me the shits.

I can't do it.

I can't survive on my own.

"She's back."

I didn't expect to find anyone here; thought they'd have all run away or been destroyed. The building itself has more or less gone, just a black, burnt-out shell of dereliction. Maybe the Boakes did catch fire after all.

I slope over to my brothers, one hiding behind the other, and onwards. Older now, harder looking, they're wiry scavengers, sinews stretched beneath nutrient-starved skin. Where eyes were once eager, they now twitch, reddened with disease. Rollo licks dried lips, haunches raised – a wolf.

"We don't want you here."

Even as he snarls I realise how much taller than me he has grown. Surely I haven't been away so long.

"Where's Leibnitz?"

I'm inching towards them – there's definitely only three of them.

"Died in the fire." Sheldon steps onto the bare earth. "Your fault."

He can't speak properly. The side of his face doesn't move. A stroke – at his age. Shit.

I sink to the ground, let them think I'm beholden.

"I can't strike a match, lads, you know that."

My remaining brothers become a blur. I have to blink repeatedly until my sight returns.

"Look again," they utter in unison.

The house – our home – it stands again. How can this be? As I watch, flames roar into life from inside the building, engulfing it in seconds.

"Get your bitch arse in there."

Rollo's grown balls. It's good. It's the right thing.

The fire is an illusion; a different kind of danger. Rollo, Sheldon and Kurtz sway with the towering reds, oranges and yellows. In the centre of the blaze, blue-black figures stumble and fall. Tom and Irene.

It cannot be so, and I say this.

"But it is, Betty. It's your work."

"No. I tore out their throats. I ran into the forest drenched in their stinking blood. It took days to get the flesh out of my teeth."

My head fills with sobs. Kurtz nudges me into the cold pyre. The cries soar in volume as I approach – and there I see it.

Tom and Irene Boakes sitting in worn but comfy matching armchairs, huge grins on insipid faces. Half-cut, as always, with bottles by their sides. Sophie Russell's on her massive cushion. Eyes as clear as the sky.

Not blind.

It's a pastoral scene of happy families. A door nudges open and in lopes a clumsy litter of puppies – all the boys, and me. I'm shy, the smallest, the runt. Where the others smile their doggie smiles, my face carries no expression whatsoever; there is nothing behind my eyes.

All sweetness and too much light in this fabrication of reality. Rollo hears my thoughts, denies them an outing.

"Keep watching."

The scenario repeats itself over time; my family growing in stature and personality whilst my own entrance is always slow, always stupid. I don't remember any of this. It is a lie. But then the re-enactment stops and I'm troubled by a flicker of recognition as the flaming house fills with weeping and wailing. The imminent death of the Queen. Panting slowly on the huge red cushion, her breath is laboured. I approach amidst orders to keep away. Sophie calls out, *Help me*, and I'm thinking she is talking directly to me. I can see she's dying. I can help with that.

I did help with that.

Little nips in all the right places.

It's all clear to me now. Nothing is as I recall it. The rebellion? It was a rebellion of one, all in my head. Helping Sophie die must have sparked something inside of me that had been dormant before that moment. The Queen's death gave me a reason to live, but it also changed my memory of how things were up until then; it warped my reality going forward, changed my understanding. I had no idea I was so damaged.

Rollo mumbles something at me and I know before I even look back into the house that he was right about the Boakes's demise. There I am, sidling into their Sophie-less living-room where they have fallen asleep with the exhaustion of grief. The wood-burner door is half open, heat escaping. Something in me wonders what would happen if the smouldering ashes, still sparking and spitting, were to fall to the ground, to ignite the carpet and catch the blankets on the Boakes's knees. I feel as detached watching this play out as I must have been when I performed it, for there I go... up to the burner door, pushing it further open. It surely must have burnt me but I seem indifferent to the pain. I raise a paw and tap, tap, tap at a hunk of wood until it falls to the floor. Boiling sap sizzles and a few sparks jump. It takes only one to catch the Crufts magazine at Irene's feet. I walk away with smoke in my throat and flames at my back.

No flesh in my teeth after all.

I did kill them, but not how I remember it.

It's *all* different to how I remember it.

The vision explodes, flames consuming the house where I grew up. As I watch myself flee, I see my brothers at my heels. Growling and baying they exile me, banish me into the woods. I must never return, or better still, die.

I didn't die.

"You should have."

I twist round to stare at their ghosts, for that's all they are, no longer real. They fade all too slowly until all that remains is a vision of broken sticks resembling broken bones strewn across the forest floor, still accusing, finding me guilty.

There is no house left here in which to find comfort. The family I'd failed to love in the right way is gone. The boys were dead-on – the fault is all mine.

I turn; the trail going back into the woods is clear. It doesn't take long to reach the dogs' graveyard where generations of canine remains have been picked well-clean; nature at her best.

The bones clatter in discordant harmony as I lay myself down upon my brothers to wait. Someone calls out, "Queen Bitch is dead".

There is no reply.

Trent

Service Dogs?

By IAN SIMMONS

Details are starting to emerge of an incident at the Trenton Services, on the edge of Dartmoor, involving what appears to be an attack by a pack of feral animals. We have reports of at least three fatalities, with the remaining people trapped inside the shop. We will keep you updated as more news comes in...

CHIHUAHUA

Mark West

The petrol gauge light had been on for five miles before Ben saw the welcome sight of a garage in the distance. It was about a mile or so away, on the crest of a small hill and beyond it he could see the rooftops of a town.

"Thank God for that," he said, willing the car to make the distance.

He'd filled the tank in Bristol, expecting it to be more than enough to get him to Plymouth but hadn't calculated for the huge traffic jams that he seemed to run into every half an hour or so. A journey that should have taken two or three hours had taken over six, and the sky was darkening as twilight eased the day along.

He passed a sign – Trenton, 2 miles – and as the road was clear, grabbed the mapbook from the passenger seat and rested it on the steering wheel. He found Trenton, on the edge of Dartmoor and only about 12 miles from Ivybridge, which was closer than he'd thought.

Trenton Services was a small independent, the Q8 station livery still visible, if faded, behind the new name. Two pumps dominated the forecourt, a Ford KA parked against one of them. The shop was beyond them, a workshop unit next to that. To the side of the station was a grassy hill and then a hedgerow that marked the start of housing.

Ben indicated, though the road was still empty, drove

onto the forecourt and parked against a pump. He got out, pulled some plastic gloves from the dispenser and unscrewed the fuel cap.

Glancing towards the shop, he saw the kid behind the counter looking towards him. Ben nodded and picked up the diesel handle as the pump whirred into life. He filled the tank and leaned on the car, looking up the hill.

Although the houses were less than a couple of hundred yards away, he couldn't hear anything other than some dogs barking. At this point in the evening he'd expect to hear lawnmowers or kids playing, perhaps music or the chatter of friends at a barbecue, but there was nothing. He looked at the shop, which had a row of dumpbins in front of it – firewood, charcoal briquettes, screenwash – and a stand holding two fire extinguishers. The station seemed to have been lifted whole from the middle of the eighties. When the pump clicked, he replaced the nozzle and fuel cap, peeled off his gloves and locked the car.

As he walked to the shop he could hear a steady growling from behind the building, like a very pissed-off dog was defending his territory. The growling got louder the closer to the door he got and he was glad to push through it into the air-conditioned interior.

A young woman, in low-cut jeans, a skinny t-shirt and bright pink flip-flops was standing at the counter. She had long blonde hair that fell to the middle of her back, secured just above her shoulders in a scrunchy. The kid behind the counter looked even younger, tall and gangly with a shock of curly brown hair and a rash of pimples across his forehead. He wore an Iron Maiden t-shirt under his 'Trenton Services' hoodie.

The shop needed a refit. The shelving on the central island was old and battered, the items on it priced with little stickers. The shelves on the wall to his right were filled with maps, newspapers and magazines and no attempt had been made to mask the covers of the ones on the top shelf. Three sun-bleached fridges stood along the back wall, advertising Coke and Pepsi. Two were filled with drinks, another with milk, sausage rolls and cold cuts of meat. Ben took out a bottle of water, checked to make sure it was in date and walked to the counter. The girl seemed to be having trouble with her credit card.

"I swear that's the pin number."

"Hey," said the kid behind the counter, "no problem."

"There is Freddy, because if this doesn't work I haven't got any cash on me."

"Trish, relax, we can sort it out."

Ben smiled and wondered how long Freddy had had his crush on Trish and whether she knew. Trish then favoured Freddy with such a bright, winning smile that Ben knew she was very much aware of it.

Freddy glanced at him. "Be with you in a minute, mate."

Trish turned her head and gave Ben her dazzling smile. "Sorry, the machine won't take my card."

"Don't worry," he said smiling back. He leaned against the counter and, in the quiet, thought he could hear the dog barking again. He wondered if Freddy had it in the back as a security measure.

Movement caught his eye and he looked towards the road as a Volvo pulled onto the forecourt, parking on the other side of the pump from Trish's KA.

"If it doesn't take it this time, I'll go and get my Dad," said Freddy, "he might be able to sort it. He was only nipping out the back to get some fuel oil, I'm supposed to be heading into town."

It was clear to Ben that Freddy wanted her to ask what his plans were, but Trish looked out of the window at the new arrivals instead. "Yeah," the kid said, carrying on as if there hadn't been a pause, "my band has a gig at the Pony and Trap."

"Really?" said Trish, still gazing out the window.

"Yeah, we're pretty good, you really should see us. I can get you in if you want, just tell the guy on the door you're with Freddy and the band."

"Uh huh."

Freddy looked along the counter to a door in the back wall, as if willing his Dad to come through. The card reader beeped and made Trish jump. Smiling, she put her card into the slot and keyed in her pin. She and Freddy looked at the display and she frowned, her shoulders slumping.

"I don't understand," she said.

Ben watched a short, slim, elderly man get out of the Volvo passenger door. He straightened up slowly, smoothing wisps of grey hair across his shining pate. He stretched his arms, then turned sharply, looking beyond Ben's car towards the slope.

"It must be the machine," said Freddy, "maybe it needs re-booting."

"I haven't got any cash on me."

"Don't worry Trish, just let me serve this fella first."

They both looked at Ben, who was surprised at the attention. "Sorry?" he said.

"The machine's not working with Trish's card, so I'll serve you first."

Trish took a step back. Outside, the old man was now moving across the forecourt towards Ben's car.

Freddy rang the value into the till, nodded at the machine and Ben slid his card into the slot. The screen wavered, then the egg-timer appeared.

"Is that a Chihuahua?" asked Trish.

Freddy looked out of the window. "Oh for Christ's sake, it's got out again."

"Does it live around here?" asked Ben.

Freddy glanced at him quickly, then back out the window. "Yeah, it's one of the houses on the hill. The stupid little thing digs its way out of the garden and wanders down here. Dad loves dogs, so says we have to make sure it doesn't get onto the road and run over. The owners don't give a shit."

The old man stopped between his Volvo and Ben's car and knelt carefully, holding his right hand out and clicking his fingers. The Chihuahua, its black and brown coat glossy, stopped and cocked its head, as if trying to work out whether he was friend or foe. It turned its head then stepped forward until it was standing right in front of the old man.

He smiled and said something. The Chihuahua launched itself at his face, springing up and clamping its wide open jaws on his nose. Shocked, the old man fell backwards, his head bouncing off the ground.

"Oh my God," said Trish.

The old man was rocking gently, trying to get up, while the dog stood on his face, its forelegs against his eyes as it gnawed his nose. Ribbons of blood ran down the man's cheeks.

"Holy shit," said Ben and moved towards the door.

"Hey," said Freddy, "wait…"

The Chihuahua reared back, bloody flesh still gripped between its teeth. The old man's head moved with the fractured jerkiness of a poorly constructed puppet.

The driver's door of the Volvo opened and a very large old lady got out, a confused expression on her face. She looked over to where the old man was – though Ben realised she couldn't see him, because of the car roof – and heard her call "Harold? Harold?" Harold didn't respond, but the Chihuahua let go of its prize and looked up.

"Harold? Are you alright?"

The old woman made her way unsteadily along the side of the car, her palms on the bodywork.

The automatic door opened and Ben stepped out into the warm evening air. He heard the growling immediately and looked to his right. Four dogs were standing at the edge of the shop. The growling came from a large Doberman with a glossy black coat. It was staring at him, ears and tail erect. Next to it was a shaggy mongrel that was looking at the old woman and baring its teeth. A sleek, off-white Jack Russell was almost dancing between the Doberman's legs, glaring at the old woman, then at the man, then back to the old woman. The last dog, standing behind the Doberman, was a long haired Golden Retriever. Its tongue was hanging out, its muzzle covered in red.

Ben took a step and the growling got louder. The Doberman took a step towards him and the Jack Russell barked excitedly. Ben took another step and so did the Doberman. The old woman looked at him, frowning.

The Doberman took another step, staring at Ben, then another, as though it was trying to get between him and the old man.

The Chihuahua yipped and danced in a circle on the old man's face.

"What's happening?" asked the old woman.

"I don't know," said Ben.

The Doberman nodded at the Golden Retriever, which barked aggressively as it moved towards Ben, licking the red from its muzzle. *Could that possibly be blood?* When the dog was about ten feet away, Ben backed into the shop and the doors shut in front of him.

"That was freaky," said Freddy.

"What's happened to the old man?" asked Trish. She was pressed against the window. "Why didn't you go and help him?"

"Did you see the other dogs?" Ben asked. He was looking out of the window, the old woman looking back at him, frowning. "That Doberman didn't want me out there, nor did the Retriever."

"They're just dogs, they bark at things."

"No," said Ben, "it wasn't that, it was…"

"I'll ring the police," suggested Freddy and he quickly dialled the number into his mobile.

Trish moved close to Ben. "Did you get the feeling the dog was organising that?"

He looked at the Doberman, then at her. "Yes," he said, "that's exactly what I thought. Did you see the muzzle of the Retriever?"

"I saw it had red on it."

"No answer," said Freddy, "that's bloody odd."

"Did you ring 999?" asked Trisha.

"No."

She glared at him. "Well why not?"

Freddy looked worried. "Well, is it an emergency?"

"You idiot," she said, "of course it is, an old man just got half his face bitten off."

"Oh, yeah." Freddy re-dialled and put the phone to his ear. "It's engaged," he said.

"What the hell's going on?" asked Trish.

The Retriever now stood in front of the door, tensed but not barking, staring into the shop. Ben saw the old woman start to make her way around the car again. Harold was lying motionless, the Chihuahua still scrambling over his face. Blood covered his right cheek, running down his neck and soaking into his shirt. Ben glanced towards the other dogs, which were fanning out as they made their way towards the Volvo.

"They're going for her," he said.

"No," said Trish, her voice low, "why would they do that?"

"I don't know," said Ben as he edged towards the door. The Retriever growled, low in its throat.

"The number's still engaged," said Freddy, sounding very confused. "I'm going to get my Dad."

"What are you doing?" asked Trish, taking a step towards Ben.

"She can't see what's happening," he said. "By the time she gets around the car, the dogs will be almost on her."

"What do you think they'll do?"

The door slid open and the Retriever barked once, loudly, then growled again. He could hear the woman calling for her husband. The Chihuahua began snapping at his nose and forehead with bared teeth.

Ben stopped at the threshold. The Retriever shifted, dropping its front legs and raising its back ones, still growling.

"Don't make eye contact," said Trish, "you're not supposed to do that."

"Yes," said Ben and looked towards the Doberman. He felt movement and for an instant was worried the Retriever had moved without him seeing, but it was just Trish.

"Hey, missus!" Ben called.

The old woman glanced at him and waved her hand, a shushing gesture.

"Hey!" called Trish. "You need to stop."

The old woman looked over. "I need you to shut up," she said, in a tight voice.

"Don't go around!

The old woman took no notice but the Doberman did.

It looked at Ben and Trish, bared its teeth and barked three times in quick succession. The Retriever started barking and Trish picked up a big packet of crisps. Without saying a word, she threw it at the dog which pounced on the pack, clamping its jaw and shaking its head savagely. It had reduced the bag to scraps in seconds and she watched it lick the crisp crumbs from the ground.

The old woman cleared the end of the car and the Doberman, head down, approached her. She looked at it, then across to Ben and Trish.

"Get back in your car!" he called.

"I need to check Harold."

"No," said Trish.

It all happened quickly. The mongrel vaulted onto the bonnet of the car, its claws scraping against the metal as the momentum carried it to the windscreen. It kicked against the glass, propelling it into the woman, hitting her in the small of the back. With a shocked cry, she fell onto her front and Ben heard her breath whoosh out of her. The mongrel clamped its jaws onto her coat and threw its head around, shredding the material. The woman tried to move, pushing herself from one side to the other, but her size and the dog prevented her from doing much.

The Jack Russell moved in and nipped at her face. The old woman screamed, bringing her hands up to shield her eyes. The dog ripped off two of her fingers. Blood sprayed across the concrete, as more seeped through the hole in her coat where the mongrel bit deeper and deeper.

Ben moved before realising he was going to, but the Retriever was ready and as he ran past, it clamped its jaws around his left ankle. His momentum pulled it off its feet before its added weight threw him sideways. He screamed, rolling across the forecourt and kicking at the dog with his other foot. Trish followed through the door, grabbed one of the fire extinguishers and stood over Ben and the dog as they writhed on the floor. The Retriever wasn't letting go, its jaws closing ever tighter, the pain so intense Ben could see black shutters closing off the extremes of his vision. He watched as Trish put the extinguisher over her head, saw the doubt in her face – that she might hit him, that she didn't want to hit the dog? – and then she pulled the catch. He just had time to close his eyes before the powder hit him. The dog released him immediately and he kicked at it, before scrambling to his feet and grabbing Trish's hand, pulling her back towards the door.

Freddy was there, holding the other fire extinguisher, pointing the hose towards the Retriever. As soon as they were through, he pushed them out of the way so the doors closed.

Safe now, intense waves of pain hit Ben and he collapsed, his leg a mass of white-hot flesh. He screamed, not knowing what to do, not really able to process what was happening.

Trish knelt beside him. "Holy shit," she said, "holy shit, what do we do?"

"Is it bad?" Ben asked.

She looked him in the eyes, glanced at his leg, then back. "Yes. There's a lot of blood."

"It's okay," said Freddy, kneeling across from Trish. He moved Ben's trouser leg gingerly and nodded at something.

"It's bleeding but not gushing and that's a good sign, it means the thing didn't get any major arteries."

"How do…?" started Trish.

He cut her off briskly. "Get some paracetamol from behind the counter." He leaned into Ben's eyeline. "Don't worry, it looks fairly clean and you're not bleeding heavily. Bleeding's good, by the way, it'll help clean out the wound."

"How do you know this?"

"My Dad's a health and safety nut, I had to go on a first aid course. More exciting than you'd think, especially the videos."

Ben smiled, in spite of the pain. "Thank you."

Trish arrived with the tablets. Freddy got a bottle of water from the fridge, opened it and propped Ben up. Ben took two tablets from Trish and washed them down with a mouthful of water.

Ben's phone rang. He pulled it out of his pocket and looked at the display. "My girlfriend," he said to them and accepted the call.

"So what now?" Trish asked Freddy. There was a smudge of blood on her chin and as she looked at Ben, tears filled her eyes. "What's going on?"

"Hello Karen" said Ben, trying to keep his voice as even as possible.

"Ben?" Karen sounded frantic. "Where are you?"

"What do you mean?"

"Haven't you been listening to the news?" He switched the mobile to loudspeaker.

"It's happening all over."

"What is?"

"The dogs! My God, don't you know?"

"Know what?" He could hear barking in the background, made tinny by the earpiece.

"Oh my God," she said, "they're at the door."

"Who is?"

Ben heard vicious barking and the line went dead. He looked up into the concerned faces of Freddy and Trish. "What's going on?" she asked.

The growling came from behind them, low and insistent. Ben tilted his head to the side and saw the Golden Retriever. It was standing at the edge of the central aisle, its head covered with white soot, one eye closed. More blood was smeared around its muzzle and one of its canines seemed to be missing.

"It's inside," he said.

The Doberman stepped around the Retriever into the aisle, staring at the three of them.

Trish, startled, unbalanced and sat down, pushing herself back until she was level with Ben's head. Freddy stood up slowly.

The growling got louder and it took Ben a moment or two to realise it was because more dogs were joining in. He watched Freddy take a step towards the Doberman, which was now baring its teeth at him.

"Oh fuck," he said.

"What?" asked Ben.

"Shit."

"What?" demanded Trisha and slowly got to her feet.

"There must be thirty of them," said Freddy. "And they're all coming in..."

Antigenex Laboratories Recruiting Security Staff After Increased Problems.

By HONEY DALE

The often controversial company has denied there are any problems in hopes to alleviate shareholder concerns. However, the latest security breach by animal rights activist will raise further questions when th AGM gathers next month. Whei. Bio-News asked for a comment we were told by Antigenex that thei operations were classified due to ii volvement with governmental agen cies. One can only assume this means military departments. Whatever is happening there the pressure is refus ing to go away. It's a science story t keep an eye on. That's one thing tha is clear at least.

In other news the discovery oi a new strand of canine DNA h hocked the scientific c

MULLIGAN STREET

D.T. Griffith

I died last night on Mulligan Street. Then a dog saved me.

A dog in a sense. A new hybrid species the doctor described to me after surgery: a coywolf. The size of a black bear. Canines aren't supposed to be that large.

It smelled like morning was approaching when I came to. My neck was limp, kind of numb. I could feel her teeth pressing into my skin, not enough to break through, but to maintain a solid grip. It didn't hurt.

She had dragged me away from the street where we were attacked. That pack of wild marauding mutts we were tracking got wise to us, it seems.

Her steaming breath carried the stench of her last fresh kill. Canine... human maybe?

I tried moving my arms and legs, twisting my torso. Nothing worked. I could look around though; enough to look past my feet and see Gary was gone. Scared off. Hell, he had to think I was already dead. I know I was. I would've left too. Josh was gone too. I wondered if they were dead and *eaten*, otherwise they would've been lying next to me.

More animals approached from the tree line lightly snapping twigs and tamping blades of grass with each elegant step. They pressed their snouts against my hair, my armpits, and my crotch while my captor tightened her grip. One barked, another responded with a defensive yelp, my captor growled in return. Her guttural tone traveled through my neck following my esophagus to my gut. It reverberated through my bones, my stomach, my nether regions. Vomiting seemed inevitable even though I could not move. I shouldn't be alive, I thought; I still think it.

A smaller coywolf the size of a German shepherd gripped my right ankle, also careful not to break skin, I wondered why. The creature's fur appeared reddish in the bits of streetlight passing through the low tree canopy, it's long, bushy tail hung low and wagged with delight.

I was their captured prey. Let the animal kingdom's natural food chain dictate my fate. It was only fair in this natural setting, a green space on the edge of a condo complex near the tree line and a brook. I could almost make out the dark plane of asphalt that made up Mulligan Street beyond the small coywolf. Yes nature, sort of, this green space. Human influenced nature.

My only crime was trespassing in this condo complex, trying to capture that pack of killer hybrids and collect the reward offered by the lab. These descendants of former house pets and wild animals, feral once more and pissed off at people. Yet we couldn't kill them, Antigenex would sue us for destroying their property.

The story we were told at the recruitment tent was an animal rights group freed the coywolves from Antigenex Laboratories. The pack had tripled in size over the past two years as they turned from nuisance to terror; the pack even took in other wild canines. Meanwhile, those liberating activists were all found mauled to death by the time the police arrived in response to Antigenex's trespass alarms.

I've never hurt any animals before, it's not my nature. Perhaps that was my saving grace with the coywolves. Those activists weren't so lucky, though; they weren't killers either. More like convenient scapegoats.

I heard a pup barking as he approached, cute little guy with an infectious dog smile; a high-pitched bark more like a coyote's than a dog or wolf's. He was jet black, unusual for a wild canine. I'm certain he was male. He sniffed around my face and nuzzled my cheek. The large female's grip on my neck finally loosened, my head dropped on the damp grass. Perhaps she had second thoughts? These creatures are not known for compassion, are they?

The release of my neck soon led to tingling in my left arm, which gave way to the itching discomfort of twigs and debris pressed into my forearm and elbow. I tried adjusting my arm with little success.

Earlier tonight the Antigenex doctor who treated me – I still haven't learned her name – said these animals are a mix of wolves, domestic dogs, and coyotes, sizes rivaling small bears. These hybrids appear in nature, but these animals were somehow genetically different. She didn't explain further, just told me I was lucky. I apparently had a *positive immune response* when the coywolf saliva made contact with my open wounds. It clotted my blood and accelerated the healing process. That's what she told me when I woke in the Antigenex facility's makeshift emergency room.

What the doctor said sort of made sense.

The black pup nuzzled me like my beagle would do at home whenever I sat on the couch. He licked my neck where the large female's teeth had gripped moments before; endorphins reacted and my vision fogged. That pup's infectious smile... my saving grace.

The grip around my ankle tightened. The large female growled at the reddish coywolf again. She was angry; the smaller reddish one didn't care. Electric tingling flowed up to my sacrum; chills followed by overwhelming heat forced their way to my brain. Muscle spasms. I remember convulsing, my limbs flailing. All I could see were points of dark gray puncturing a light gray cloud that progressively grew darker. They're doing it, I thought, they're eating me now. I could feel my legs for a moment. This was the end, I could have prayed to god if I had one I believed in... one I could have trusted amongst these hybrid monsters... or pray to a new god. This canine's god.

Prey.

I could twitch my right foot. The bloodied toe of my Converse came into view beyond the gray fog. I tried to move it again as the mutt clamped down on my ankle. My foot lay still. Lifeless.

I hoped the police would show. I hoped that Gary or Josh had the bright idea of calling for help if they were still alive. I hoped they were alive. Real help. The police kind of help. The firefighters and medics. Something. Animal control. Just not the Antigenex Lab folks paying the bounties. They saw us trackers as expendable. Now I understood why. We're their guinea pigs. I was in the middle of a freakin' city and there was nobody around. All by design.

I kept working at my ankle. I could feel my muscles move a little, but my foot wouldn't respond. The reddish coywolf growled and another wash of hot energy rushed through my leg and consumed my body. The last thing I saw as I passed out was my Converse falling away from me.

I opened my eyes and it was midday I think. A woman wearing a blue windbreaker held her ear to my chest. The Antigenex doctor.

"He's alive," she called out. "Can you talk?"

A gurgling sound came from my throat. I tried to move my jaw, but it felt wrong – hot and stiff. I managed to hiss a negative.

"We have a triage unit downtown, we're taking you there now," she said, her voice filled with urgency and remorse.

I tried to move again, this time my arms responded. I held up my left hand and then checked my right – missing three fingers on the right: pinky, ring and middle. Stumps that had clotted, lucky I didn't bleed out.

The woman gently put my hands down by my sides. "Don't move," she said, "I don't want you hurting yourself any worse than you are."

I lifted my right leg just enough to see my foot was gone at the ankle. How did I not bleed out? How am I alive? She dressed my right leg in a tight bandage then tended to my hand.

"You are lucky to be alive," she said. "The saliva's healing properties actually worked, your blood clotted quickly. You lived."

Gary came into view, standing over me. "Hey ol' friend, glad we found you. We're gonna get you better, okay?" He blotted my forehead with a rag. "You're gonna be okay."

"This will help you with the pain," the doctor said, preparing an IV needle. She spoke in a hushed tone to Gary.

"This is all my fault." She let out a big sigh as she injected me. "I can't take another tragedy like this. More dead coywolves. This wasn't the plan."

Gary said something about Josh waiting for him back at the triage. They thought they saw me die when a large beast grabbed me by the neck and flung me around.

I could swear I had died.

They lifted me onto a stretcher and carried me to a blue van with the familiar *AGX Labs* logo on the side. As my head lolled to the side I could see the black pup was injured and restrained in a harness. A man wearing a blue jacket led the animal to a pickup truck outfitted with a large cage in back. The scent of death was impossible to ignore, but I didn't care at that point. The reddish coywolf lay still near the street, my shoe-encased foot still in its mouth. I tried to tell Gary my foot was over there, but nothing came out. I don't know what killed and injured the coywolves, but there was no sign of my former captor, the giant female.

What little was left inside me faded with the injection. I knew right away I was done.

I am done.

Good Doggy or Bad Boy?

The police have yet to comment on the attack at Trenton services but locals have spoken of horrific fights.

***

Does Your Dinner Meat Quality Standard?

Black market meat is driving up prices for the family butcher. It may seem like a bargain and a handy slice off the weekly shop but do illegal foods really help the household budget in the long run? Leaders in the butcher's union have also suggested the meat sold from the back of a lorry or in some untrustworthy markets may actually be harmful to the consumer. Though cases of food poisoning have yet to be recorded. Though Len McCartney a local butcher says it's only a matter of time until we see people falling ill, or even worse, dying.

Burger Van

Michael Bray

Trent looked at the bag of meat, and then turned his attention back to the scrawny rat of a man called Gable at the other side of the table. "I'll give you an even hundred."

Gable shifted, and flicked his eyes to his bulky colleague who was lingering in the shadows. "Nah, man. Two hundred. That was the deal. We had an agreement."

"You promised me sixty pounds. There's only forty here."

Gable again glanced to his friend and scratched his grubby cheek. "We had, uh, distribution problems."

"Not my fault," Trent said, holding firm and folding his arms.

"Come on man, you're killing me here," Gable said, staring at the vacuum packed bag of pink mincemeat on the table.

Trent feigned disinterest, throwing in an exaggerated sigh for good measure. "Maybe we should just forget it if we can't agree a price."

Gable squirmed and said nothing.

"Look," Trent said, leaning on the table, flexing his thick forearms. "We both know I'm your only customer for this. Based on where you had me come out to meet you, you're keen to keep this under the radar. You also know that if it's good quality, I'll buy more from you. You *can* get more, right?"

"Yeah, I can get more," Gable said, cheek twitching as he continued to look for something to focus his eyes on.

"Alright, then you scratch my back and I'll scratch yours. Give me this for a hundred, and as long as it's good, I'll buy the next batches off you going forward for one fifty per sixty pounds. Not forty. Not fifty. Sixty, or no deal. Got it?"

Another glance to his shadowy friend and Gable nodded his head. "Yeah, alright man, you got yourself a deal."

Trent handed over the cash and picked up the bag. "Two weeks today. Sixty pounds of meat for a hundred and a half." He turned and disappeared into the shadows of the warehouse before Gable or his friend could say or do anything else.

THREE MONTHS LATER

The smell of frying onions punctuated what was shaping up to be a glorious summer day. Trent's burger van had already established a good reputation for the quality of its food, but now people were flocking to sample his new product. He looked at the people lined up three deep as he placed two new burger patties on the grill, which sizzled and hissed. He had managed to secure a prime location on Anson's Park, a thoroughfare for both local business people looking to get a bite to eat as well as regular pedestrian traffic who might want a quick snack on their way through the park. As busy as he was, it was frightening to think how a forgotten tax bill had almost wiped out the business which had been in his family for three generations. None of those who came before had seen anything like the success Trent was currently enjoying. It had been a make or break situation. Either find a way to cut costs, or go under. That, however, was easier said than done, and for a while it looked like the business was about to go belly up until a chance encounter with an old friend of his from high school, Richie Orkney, led to Trent telling him all about his plight. Richie had listened then said he might know someone who could help.

Cheap meat, he'd said. Good quality at a fraction of the price. For Trent, it was the one way out that might, just might, pay off. Richie had set up the first meeting and the business arrangement was completed. The last three months had been spent slowly but surely climbing out of the red and back into the black. He couldn't help but smile as he put another half dozen patties on the grill, sending more of that delicious smell billowing towards him and, more importantly, his customers. He was happy. Life was certainly on the up.

"How was your day?" Claire said as he walked into the house and shrugged out of his jacket.

"Busy. Something smells good," he said, giving her a quick peck on the cheek.

"Chicken. It'll be ready in half an hour."

"Sounds good to me. Where's the Munchkin?"

Claire smiled as he started up the steps. "She's in her room. Don't be too long up there, dinner will be ready soon."

Trent went upstairs and walked down the landing towards his daughter's room. He paused outside the door, her name, Holly, painted on the wood in pink. He could hear her having imaginary conversations with her toys, oblivious to his presence.

He poked his head into the bedroom. "Boo."

"Daddy," she squealed, running towards him. He picked her up and she hugged him tightly around the neck.

"How's my little munchkin today?" he said, setting her down.

"I'm good, Mr Tickles isn't playing nice," she said, frowning at the toys on the carpet.

"I heard that from outside. Which one is Mr Tickles?"

She pointed to a white bear on the floor. "That one."

"Who's the other guy?" Trent asked, nodding to the purple plush toy beside it.

"Daddy, that one's not a guy, it's a girl. She's Lady Pam."

"Oh, Lady Pam is it?" Trent repeated. "Then I apologise to the good lady for calling her a guy."

"Do you want to play for a while?" Holly asked.

"Maybe later. Dinner's almost ready. You wash up soon, okay? Make sure Mr Tickles and Lady Pam do the same."

"I will, Daddy." He kissed her on the head then went into his bedroom, sitting on the edge of the bed and kicking his shoes off. He took his phone out of his pocket and dialled the number he had stored simply as 'New Supplier.' It was answered on the third ring.

"It's me," Trent said. "I need more meat. How soon can you get me some?"

He listened as the voice on the other end of the line answered him. "Alright, Sunday in the usual place." He hung up the phone and put it in on the dresser. Life for Trent Billingham and his family was good, and if things were to carry on the way they were, it would only get better.

For the next fortnight business continued to grow, to the point where he and Claire had been discussing hiring an extra set of hands to help with the seemingly endless intake of customers. It was the middle of the lunchtime rush, and as always, he was swamped with customers. Trent flipped a burger onto a bun, loaded it with cheese and salad, then folded it into a paper napkin and handed it to a customer.

"Thanks," the portly recipient said as he took a bite. "These are delicious, my friend, really good."

"I appreciate that," Trent said as he checked the other half dozen burgers which were cooking.

"I come here pretty much every other day now. Seems like you have a bit of an admirer too." The customer said around a mouthful of food.

Trent looked at him and frowned, unsure what he was getting at. The man swallowed down his food, then jabbed a fat thumb over his shoulder. "Looks like someone can smell what you're cookin' over here."

Trent looked past the man and the crowd. There was a tan coloured dog on the opposite side of the street. It was sitting on its haunches, watching him, nose twitching. He wasn't sure of the breed but had suspected it was a retriever of some kind.

"Looks like even he's heard about how good the food is here."

Trent nodded and was about to ask the man if he'd seen the dog before when another customer asked for ketchup. Trent gave it to him, then checked on the burgers. For the next two hours he worked, until the crowds finally began to thin out, more convinced than ever that they would need to hire more help. It was only when he found the time to really look around that he saw the dog was still there and didn't look to have moved. It had been joined by two others of its kind. A small, scruffy terrier with overgrown fur, and a black and white border collie. All three were staring at him.

"They've been there for a while."

Trent turned his attention to the customer standing by the van, half eaten burger in one hand. "Looks like they're hungry," the man added.

"Yeah," Trent said. He took a burger patty out of the fridge and broke a piece off, tossing it to the dogs. He expected them to come running, perhaps fight over the morsel they had been waiting all day for, but none of them moved. They simply stayed where they were and watched him. He threw another piece, this one landing close to the terrier. It ducked its head and smelled the offering, then looked back at Trent, the meat left untouched.

"Eh, maybe not. Animals, eh? Strange things. Take it

easy, buddy," the customer said, grinning and going on his way.

"Yeah, take it easy," Trent muttered as he looked at the dogs. He watched them for a while, curious as to why they wouldn't take the food, then shrugged it off. The customer had been right. Animals were strange things; besides it was getting late, and he wanted to get home. He started to close up, cleaning down the surfaces, stocking the drinks fridges and taking his inventory for the next day to ensure he could meet the demand for his product. Just before he locked up the van, he looked out over the park for the dogs, but they had gone, leaving the fleshy, pink meat behind where he had thrown it. Unsure why it made him so uneasy, he closed up the van and drove to the storage unit. Despite it being another profitable day, he didn't really feel happy. A subtle uneasiness had started to creep into him which he couldn't explain. He dropped the van off at the storage unit, then walked the two miles home. When he arrived he was feeling a bit better and slightly ashamed for letting such a simple thing bug him. He opened the door and went inside, relieved to have another day behind him. Before he could get his coat off, Claire hurried into the hallway, the expression on her face telling him that something was wrong.

"Where have you been? I've been trying to call you," she said, wringing her hands together.

"You have?" he pulled his phone out of his jeans pocket. "Shit, battery must have died on me. What's wrong?"

"It's Holly. She was playing out back and a dog got through the gate and bit her on the arm."

Trent's breath caught in his throat. "Is she alright?" he managed.

"It's fine, it's just a nip really, but she's scared. I've been asking you to fix that gate for weeks, Trent. It's not safe"

"I know, I know. I'll do it this weekend, okay? It's just been so busy at work lately I haven't had the time."

"I know, I'm not taking it out on you, I just...she was really upset."

"Where is she?"

"She's upstairs watching a DVD."

"Frozen again?"

"Not this time. Finding Nemo."

"Nemo, huh? Alright, I'll go up and see her. Sorry about the gate. I'll definitely do it at the weekend. No more delays."

"Its fine," Claire replied, hugging him. "Just go see her. She'll feel better knowing you're here."

He went upstairs, trying to ignore any suggestion that the events at work and at home were linked.

"Hi, daddy," Holly said as he entered the bedroom.

"Hey, Munchkin. How's the arm?"

"Okay I guess," she said as he sat on the edge of the bed. "Mom made me a bandage."

She thrust her arm towards him, showing it to him.

"She did a great job. What are you watching?" he asked, glancing at the TV.

"Finding Nemo."

"Finally seen enough of Frozen, huh?"

She sat up and grabbed his hand, catching him by surprise. "Daddy, I'm scared," she whispered.

"There's nothing to be scared of. Some dogs just don't like people that's all, even if they do look cute."

"It's outside, Daddy. It's watching me."

"Holly, come on," he said, laying her back down and pulling the blankets up. "It's not watching you. That poor animal was probably as scared as you were. Sometimes, when an animal feels threatened, they attack. It's not personal."

"It's out there, Daddy, I know it is," she insisted, glancing towards the window.

"I promise you, it isn't."

"Will you check for me? Please, Daddy?"

"Alright, if it will make you feel better," he said as he walked over to the window and looked out into the street.

Nope. Nothing there.

That was what he intended to say, even expected to say, however as he looked down into the sodium lamp bathed street below, the three dogs from the park were staring at the house. With them were a half dozen others, various breeds and sizes.

"Can you see it, Daddy? Is it there?" Holly asked, her voice distant and detached.

"No, there's nothing there, Munchkin. Nothing at all," he mumbled as he struggled to digest what he was looking at. He stepped back and closed the curtains, hoping Holly wouldn't notice the way his hands were shaking. He walked back across the room and kissed her on the head. "Come on now, you watch your film and forget all about this dog stuff, okay? I'm going to fix the gate at the weekend so this won't happen again."

"Alright," she mumbled, clearly not convinced.

"Tell you what, how about I get changed then make you a hot chocolate?"

"Yay!" she squealed, instantly brought out of her gloom in the way children were by good news.

"Alright then. You just promise me you'll stay right there and watch the film, okay? No talking to Mr Tickles, no looking out of the window. Promise?"

"I promise," she said, grinning at him and giving the animated fish on the television screen her full attention.

"Good girl," Trent said, gently closing the door. Safely out of sight, he dropped his calm demeanour and hurried to his bedroom, almost tripping over the foot of the bed as he headed for the window. He swept the curtain aside, glaring out into road below, but the dogs had gone, the streets now empty. He stared anyway, trying to see if they might be hiding between the other houses or in the shadows.

Did I imagine it? Did I look out there and my brain was somehow tricked into seeing those dogs because they were already in my mind?

He supposed it was possible, but it didn't *feel* like something he'd imagined. Even if he had imagined the dogs in the street, the ones at the van that had been watching him were *definitely* real. Other people had seen them before he had, and even if it was possible that he'd somehow mingled the two experiences up in his brain (he had, after all, been overworking recently), there was no reason he would manifest them now outside his own house. It just made no sense. Confused and uncertain what to believe, he changed and decided it was best not to mention it to Claire. Not until he had had some time to think about it. Even so, for the first time in almost ten years he walked around the house and double checked all the doors and windows to make sure they were securely locked.

Just to be on the safe side.

There were seven dogs the next day. Trent stood in his van, going through the motions of the morning preparation and trying to ignore them. He had barely slept, and had spent the previous night dozing in the dark in his armchair, baseball bat draped across his knees, every single noise from the house starting him awake, making him think there was something inside. Claire had asked him if he was alright, and because he still didn't have the inclination to tell her what was happening, he had given a vague story about coming down with a bug of some kind. One thing the sleepless night had done was give him a little time to think about what might be happening and why and although he had no proof, he was determined to find out. The day went on, and Trent went through the routine of his work in the same kind of detachment that had been with him since he saw the dogs out of Holly's bedroom window. By the time the mid-afternoon rush arrived, there were fifteen dogs watching him. He glared at them as he cooked, that detached nausea still surging through him as he served his customers, barely able to muster up the usual level of banter he had become known for. He wondered why nobody had come to gather them or round them up, or why no warden had come. He considered calling them and yet he couldn't bring himself to do it. Not until he was sure of what was happening and couldn't deny any longer that, for whatever reason, the dogs were interested in him.

He stared at the dogs, and the dogs looked right back at him.

Slowly, he had started to put the pieces together, and was perhaps starting to understand what was happening. He glanced at the dog, the first one that had noticed at the burger van. It sat at the front of the pack, drool hanging from its jaws, eyes black and emotionless. That was when he first felt it.

Fear.

Honest to God real fear, which was far removed from the horror film scare he associated with the word. This was real, visceral, a primal emotion which he knew until that point he had never experienced before.

Even though they were technically domestic animals – many of them were wearing collars and tags – there was a primal aggression that he could sense within the pack of dogs even from the relative safety of the van. He suspected that even though there were a lot of people around, none were approaching the animals to stroke them or to check if they had owners nearby. If anything, people were giving them a wide berth, doing their best to ignore the animals and skirting past them as if they had some kind of contagious disease. Trent suspected that, like him, people could sense the aggression. He wondered which one of them it was that had bitten his daughter. He suspected it was the one he referred to as their leader, the tan coloured retriever, only because that one was the first to come to him. He couldn't concentrate, all he could do was look at the animals and try to figure out what he should do.

He slammed the burger flipper down on the grill. "We're closed," he hissed.

"Hey, I'm still waiting for my food," one customer said, frowning at the sudden outburst.

"I said we're closed, are you deaf?" Trent fired back, still unable to tear his eyes away from the animals. "You must all be blind. Don't tell me you can't see them over there staring."

"Hey, take it easy, buddy," the customer said, holding his palms up.

"They came to my house, did you know that?" Trent said, narrowing his eyes and staring at his audience. "To my fucking house!"

People started to back away. He could only imagine how he must look to them, sweating and wild eyed. The burger flipper who had finally flipped. If there was something the public knew well to avoid it was a crazy person, and almost as one they melted away, deciding that as nice as the food may be, it wasn't worth it to stick around and see what the man selling them might do next. He didn't care about that now though. All he could think about were the dogs.

"Go on, get out of here. Get the fuck out!" He was screaming at the dogs, but the customers thought he was referring to them, increasing their distance from him and the van. The dogs, however, didn't move. They continued to sit and stare at him. Trent was almost sure he could sense some kind of arrogance there. He felt nausea sweep over him, and he swayed on his feet, sure he was going to collapse. With a trembling hand he closed the shutter, convincing himself it was because he was closing up and not because he was afraid. Somehow it was worse not being able to see them. He saw it play out in his mind's eye like a low budget horror film. The dogs would come now he was alone, perhaps as a portentous soundtrack raised the viewer's tension in the background. The dogs would then wage some kind of assault on his van as he cowered in the back, defying the laws of science as they did. It was ridiculous, of course. They were dogs, not monsters. He stood there in the dark and listened, waiting for it to begin. But there was no attack, no hollow padding of feet on steel as they clambered all over the van. Just the ragged sound of his own breathing. Eventually, Trent opened the rear door and poked his head out. The park was quiet and bathed in mid-afternoon sun. The dogs had dispersed, gone to wherever they went when they weren't harassing him. He held his breath and listened. Aside from the breeze and the distant sound of children playing elsewhere in the park, there was a sense of utter normalcy, which under the circumstances made him feel even more uncomfortable. Even so, he knew they were still out there somewhere. Watching him. Waiting for him. He climbed out of the van and locked the back door, unable to resist glancing over his shoulder to make sure they weren't behind him.

In the movies they would be under the van, waiting there to bite your ankle when you least expect it, and then attack in a pack as that ominous soundtrack built into a crashing, screeching crescendo as the victim was finally taken, fake blood spilling out of his mouth as he screamed and gargled into the camera..

He tried not to think about it, still trying to tell himself that things like this didn't happen in real life. He forced himself not to run as he moved towards the cab of the van, hoping that if they were watching they would see he wasn't intimidated. Once he was safely inside, he relaxed a little, knowing he couldn't put off trying to find out any longer. He took his phone out of his pocket, dropped it, and then snatched it up off the cab floor. He tried calling Richie, intending to ask him what he knew about the supplier he had put him in touch with. Richie's line rang and remained unanswered. Frustrated, he punched in the number for the supplier directly, unsure if he was more angry or afraid at how things were playing out.

"Yeah?" Gable said as he answered the phone. He sounded drowsy, and Trent was sure he was either high or half asleep.

"It's Trent Billingham. I need to talk to you about our arrangement."

"What about it?"

"Not over the phone. Face to face. Be at the warehouse

in an hour," he said, hoping the fear didn't come through across the phone.

"I don't have any stock yet, buddy. We agreed on next week."

"I know what we agreed. This isn't about that. One hour. If you're not there, consider our arrangement finished." He hung up and tossed his phone on the passenger seat, then leaned his head on the steering wheel and closed his eyes.

This isn't happening. This can't be happening. He repeated it in his head over and over, hoping that repetition would make it so, but as much as he tried, the facts said otherwise. He started the van and set off towards the meeting point.

The warehouse was by the waterfront, and looked infinitely less intimidating during the day. It had been abandoned six months earlier, and was already covered in graffiti. When Trent arrived, Gable was already there, leaning on the hood of a filthy Ford sedan and smoking a cigarette. Trent pulled up beside him and clambered out of the van, pleased to see that his oafish bodyguard wasn't present.

"Hey man, if you want more meat I—"

Trent grabbed him by the jacket and slammed him into the side of the van. "Where does it come from? Where do you get it?"

"Hey, back off, man." Trent didn't move. He kept Gable pinned there, squirming trying to get free, cigarette dangling from his lip. "I'm just the middle man. I didn't know anything about it. Fucking let go of me."

"But you know what it is, don't you?" Trent said, even to himself his voice sounded a few octaves too high.

"It's meat, man. You asked for meat and that's what you got."

"What kind of meat? What animal?" Trent was now glaring, teeth gritted as he tried to contain his anger. He realised he must look insane, and stifled the bizarre urge to laugh.

"You wanted cheap. You got cheap. You were happy. We all were, I don't know what you want from me?"

"Answer me, or I swear to god I'll do something I might regret," Trent growled, surprised at how aggressive he was being. It wasn't in his nature to be confrontational, but he supposed fear changed a man.

"Dog, man. It's dog meat," Gable blurted.

Trent let him go, Gable staggered away, straightening his jacket. "Just strays, man. None that anyone will miss. What the fuck did you expect? Fucking Angus beef or somethin'?"

Trent leaned on Gable's car, feeling as if someone had just punched him in the gut. "You've no idea what you've done."

"I don't know why you're so pissed, man. They're just dogs. Just dumb dogs."

"Not that dumb," Trent muttered as he opened the door to his van.

"Hey man, you still want the delivery next week right? I've already told my guy you had made a commitment to buy. He's sourcing the stock right now."

Trent ignored him and put the van into reverse,

turned and raced away from the warehouse, a rooster tail of dust behind him. Gable didn't matter to him now. He knew why the dogs were watching him, and even that was secondary to the one thought which reverberated over and over in his brain and made the fear he had felt before increase tenfold.

They know where I live.

He had considered driving the van all the way home, but knew that such a random and irrational act would only alarm his family and make them ask questions he was in no position to answer. Even though his instinct screamed otherwise, he dropped the van off at the lockup and set off walking home, resisting the urge to run, nerves on edge at every sound. He saw an old woman walking a poodle and almost screamed, even when this particular canine paid him no attention whatsoever. His nerve endings shredded, he picked up his pace, desperate to get home.

The first dog didn't start to follow him until a half mile from the house. It was the tan retriever, the very first dog that had started to watch him. To see it sent Trent into a blind panic, and he increased his pace. The dog kept its distance, trotting along behind him. He could feel its eyes boring into his back.

As Trent neared the house, more of them came. Out of side streets, hopping over fences and falling in behind the retriever. The fear was so intense he could taste it, but knew he couldn't break into a run, not yet at least. He was overweight and unfit and knew they would chase him down with ease if he tried to escape them.

He turned into his street and could see his house three quarters of the way down. The temptation was too great and he broke into a sprint, breath ragged, arms and legs pumping. This was fear, and it drove him on. The dogs gave chase, a snarling, barking mass of legs and teeth. Trent realised he had misjudged both the distance and his fitness, and knew he wasn't going to make it. His world was filled with the deafening barking of his pursuers as he pushed way beyond his limits. He risked a glance over his shoulder, immediately wishing he hadn't. The dogs were less than fifteen feet behind. His feet tangled, and for a split second he was sure he was going to pitch over. He pin-wheeled his arms, knowing that to fall would mean death. Somehow he stayed upright, the frightened voice in his head screaming at him to get inside, to get to his family. He reached his driveway, the snarling animals at his heels. Already exhausted, the slight uphill gradient seemed impossibly steep, his exhausted body and overworked heart refusing to push any further. Somehow he found the will to push on, more out of fear of what would happen to him than anything else. At his back, the dogs clattered into each other, their sheer numbers working against them, buying him the few precious seconds he needed to get to the door. He fumbled at the handle. Once. Twice. They were on him now, closing down on him. He wondered how it would feel as their teeth penetrated his flesh, when he was decimated on his own driveway. He could imagine how it would look. He would look like something that had been thrown through a wood chipper, all blood and pulp with no recognisable features.

Holly will see it.

He was spared from his morbid train of thought by the door clicking open, his fumbling finally granting him access. He fell onto the hall carpet on his hands and knees, and kicked the door shut just as the first dog slammed into the wood. Trent lay there, panting and drenched in sweat, breath rasping in his throat. Claire appeared in the hallway, staring at him in disbelief.

"What happened to yo—"

"Where's Holly," he said between ragged breaths.

"Jesus, Trent, what's wrong with—"

"Holly! Where is she?" he screamed, knowing it was too late now to hide how afraid he was.

"She's playing out back."

He lurched to his feet, barging past Claire and through the hallway.

"Trent, what the hell's going on?"

"Pack a bag for you and Holly. Enough for a few days," he said over his shoulder as he went through the kitchen. The back door was open, and he could hear Holly outside. He prayed the dogs wouldn't be there, hoping that his luck would hold for just a little longer.

His daughter sat in the backyard on the floor playing with Mr Tickles and Lady Pam. From his vantage point, he could see over the fence and back gate to the street outside. The dogs were there, lined up and watching him, noses twitching, lips curled back from teeth.

Trent's plan had been to be gentle and not scare Holly,

the idea gone as soon as he saw the dogs. "Holly, inside now. Come on," he screamed.

She looked at him, frown on her tiny face. "What is it, Daddy?"

"I said in, now!" he ran down the steps, hating that he had made her cry. He picked her up and carried her back towards the house, leaving the toys behind.

"Trent, what the hell is wrong with you?" Claire said as she stood and stared at him. He set Holly down and she ran to her mother, sobbing as Claire scooped her up.

"No time to explain. Have you packed a bag?"

"Trent, you're scaring me."

"Forget it, there's no time now. Go get in the car."

"Trent..."

"Please, just do it," he screamed as Holly's cries increased.

"Trent, you're scaring her."

"Just get in the fucking car!" he said, slamming his fist on the worktop. Holly screamed and buried her head in her mother's neck.

Shaken by his outburst, Claire nodded and moved to the side door in the kitchen which opened onto the garage. She put Holly down and opened the back door, then started to strap her into the child seat. "We still need things. Clothes for me and Holly. What's this about, Trent?" she said, now also crying.

"I'll explain later. Right now we need to go."

"You're in some kind of trouble, aren't you? Please just talk to me."

"Not now. Please, hurry up."

She knew him well enough to know not to argue when he was so on edge. Instead, she did as he asked, getting in the passenger seat as Holly's cries finally started to subside. Trent got into the driver's seat and glanced across at Claire. "Close that window."

"What?"

"Please, just close it. Just until we get out of the street."

She did as he asked, and half turned towards him. He could see that she was afraid of him and hated it. "What is this, Trent?"

"You'll see," he said as he started the engine then pressed the control for the garage door. It rolled open, much too slowly for his liking. He stared in the mirrors, waiting to see if the dogs would try to attack the car. He reversed out into the driveway, fighting the urge to do so at speed because his daughter was in the back. He had expected to see a lawn full of dogs baying for blood, waiting to finish what they started.

Trent frowned. The street was empty.

"What am I supposed to be looking for?" Claire said, confusion replacing fear for the time being.

"Never mind," he muttered, then pressed the button on the car keys, closing the garage door, then reversed out into the street. As he drove away, an upset wife demanding answers beside him and confused child in the back, he was surprised that rather than make him feel better, the lack of dogs made him feel infinitely worse.

Claire's mother lived five miles away in a quiet, quaint neighbourhood. The drive over had been tense, Claire asking questions he was unable to answer. His priority had been to get his family safe, but knew it was only a temporary measure. The dogs had followed him to work, and they had followed him home. It stood to reason that they would follow him there too if he allowed it. He helped Claire get Holly out of the car, then went to climb back into the driver's side.

"What are you doing?" Claire asked, sending Holly up to the front door where her confused and surprised grandmother stood.

"I need to go back and get some things for you. Some for me too."

"You said it was dangerous. The way you acted…"

"It's fine. I'll explain later. Just go inside, wait for me here and I'll come back soon, okay?"

"You can't do this, Trent. You can't just leave it like this."

He got into the car and closed the door, staring straight ahead, knowing that if he looked her in the eye, he would break and not go, then be resigned to waiting until the dogs came for him. "Just stay here. I'll be back," he muttered.

He reversed the car out of the driveway, hating himself for leaving the way he had, and wishing he could explain that it was all for their own good. He drove away from the house, wondering if even now the dogs were out there in the dark, watching him.

He parked the car at the end of the street, hoping that he could get in and out quietly on foot before the dogs knew he had even returned. He had a gun in a shoebox on top of the wardrobe in the bedroom, and although harming any sort of animal was something he would never do, this situation was different. Despite the fear that seemed to have consumed him over the last few days, there was now a calmness to Trent as he stood looking down the street. It was quiet, most homes with windows ablaze with golden light as families settled down for dinner or to watch television. He walked towards his house, notably the only one still shrouded in darkness. It looked like a tomb of some kind, a place of death born from a situation of his making. As he approached, the dogs fell in behind him, again appearing from gardens and over fences. Trent didn't run, not at first, but as more joined the following pack the aggression within them increased. They began to growl and snap at his heels, and Trent couldn't help but break into a run, sprinting towards the house. He fumbled for the door in an almost carbon copy of the earlier incident, grateful the door hadn't been locked in the haste of their fleeing. He shouldered it open and slammed it closed, screaming in rage and frustration. He wondered if he could go through with it, if he could point the gun at those animals and pull the trigger. He wasn't sure, but had become desperate enough to try, especially with his family's safety at risk. He looked through the spyhole on the door, the world outside a warped globe showing the garden and driveway. The dogs that had followed him sat on the lawn, staring at the door, blocking his exit.

"If that's the way you want it, then that's the way we'll

do it," he muttered, and was about to turn and head upstairs when he heard the low, throaty growl from behind.

Trent froze, and turned slowly around, his back pressed to the door. The dogs were everywhere. Standing on every surface, lining the corridors. Down the hall he could see the back door still open. In his hurry to flee, he hadn't closed it when he'd brought Holly inside. Trent couldn't even guess how many dogs were in the house. He guessed at least fifty, probably more. All of them were staring at him, eyes without any form of emotion. Directly in front of him was the tan retriever.

"I didn't know," Trent whispered. "If I'd known I wouldn't have bought it. I'll stop now, I promise, do you understand me? It's over."

The dogs didn't attack, or move. They simply stared and waited.

"I'm trying to tell you I'm sorry!" he screamed, blinking tears which rolled down his cheeks. "What else do you want from me? What do you want me to do?"

The dogs waited, all of them now growling, muscles tense and waiting to pounce. Trent was starting to sweat now, his heart a thundering tempo. A pain in his chest, a twinge at first then radiating up into his jaw. He staggered and a few of the dogs moved back. Not the retriever though. He stood his ground, watching Trent with black eyes.

He fell to the ground. The dogs watching as he lay there, unable to move, unable to do anything but stare and wait for the attack to come.

A heart attack. Ironic, really.

He had been warned about this by his doctor. Change your diet. Get more exercise. Don't work so hard. He'd intended to follow the instructions, but it was always tomorrow, or next week. Now it was too late. He lay on his back completely immobilised. The retriever padded over to him, its snout inches from Trent's face, man and beast locked in eye contact. Trent was already fading, the life ebbing away from him. One final rational thought came to mind as he thought of his wife and daughter. *I never told them I love them before I left.* He blinked once then took one final shallow breath. The dogs waited, staring at the dead man on the floor. The retriever made a sound, a half cough, half snort, then one by one the other dogs began to file out of the house the way they had come, through the kitchen and out of the back door, leaping over the small fence or squeezing through the gaps in the iron gate, returning to their masters, to homes and families who took them for granted and had no idea of the intelligence they possessed. Only the retriever remained. It lifted a paw and nudged Trent's chest, watching for a reaction. Trent didn't move, his dead eyes continuing to stare into oblivion. Satisfied, the retriever slowly turned and walked towards the back door. It turned and took one last look at Trent, then ran through the yard, clearing the fence in a single leap and away.

Into the night.

Shawbury

August 18, 2018

Dognapping In Sleepy Town

Local dog owners are being urged to keep an eye out for gangs of dognappers who are believed to be operating in the area. Unconfirmed reports suggest that the canines are being groomed for use in illegal dogfights. Police refused to comment on these rumours which have been circling for months nor to confirm the involvement of Richard 'Beako' Beakman who is believed to be helping with their enquiries. Chief Superintendent Thomas said "We are aware of a number of incidents where dogs have gone missing recently. We ask the public to be ever vigilant and to report anything suspicious to us here at Shawbury Police Station."

A Dog is for Death

Phil Sloman

The crowd was eager for blood. Blood and money.

Close to one hundred people had crammed inside the ballroom in an oppressive mixture of heat and aggression. It was a long way from the glamour and sophistication of The Ritzy's heyday, when the likes of Valerie Targus and Brian Beauchamps had danced the Viennese Waltz across the lacquered ballroom floor, drawing applause from an enraptured audience. But those days were long gone. A botched insurance job had seen the building burn brightly back in the seventies leaving a blackened shell and no one prepared to foot the bill for renovations. It was in this mix of darkness and decay that a different form of *entertainment* had taken hold on the dancefloor of the derelict building.

"I'll 'ave a monkey on the black one."

"Fifty nicker on Satan!"

Bets were barked out indiscriminately. People jostled for position at the head of a shambolic queue where muscle overrode manners. Money changed hands for slips of paper marked with Beako's moniker. Beako had been running the Tote at these 'gatherings' for the best part of two years. He was a small, hunched man possessed of a disproportioned nose which gave him his nickname. Portly was the polite way of describing his general physique. Rotund would have been another. Most would call him a fat cunt but not to his face. He had limited appreciation for insults, especially those made against him. The protection he paid for made certain that everyone knew it, and he wasn't averse to getting his hands dirty if the need arose. Those who were unfamiliar with Beako's predilection for manners never made the same mistake twice.

"Book's closed. Book's closed," shouted Beako with an excess of theatre, still writing slips and pocketing money as the handlers prepared themselves in what haphazardly constituted a ring. A circle of ragged chairs had been looped together with ropes misappropriated from the local building sites. The cloth of the seats had been ripped wide open over the years, encouraging yellow foam to spill out. Goons stood with handheld Tasers around the edge of the ring, packing enough volts to stop the most ferocious of beasts or men.

The crowd bayed louder as Beako's words repeatedly rose above the throng, each spectator, man and woman alike, anticipating the start of their evening's entertainment. Their chanting escalated as Beako waddled his way to the edge of the ring, his thugs forcing a path through the crowd for him. With effort, Beako clambered onto one of the ringside chairs, giving him height over those who had come out for the night. The sight of Beako gathering his estimable bulk onto the torn seating would have met with laughs and caterwauling anywhere else, but this was Beako's theatre and no one would mock him here. Standing tall, he surveyed his public, reading the salivating faces of his punters. He recognised them all, each one vetted before being allowed into his premises. At the back he saw Tony Chapman holding up his phone and filming proceedings. Beako made a mental note to have his protection pay Tony a visit before the night was out. If Tony was lucky, his fingers would heal in time for Christmas, if not, well Beako didn't care much either way.

"Ladeez and gen'l'men." Beako lifted his hands above his head, calling for silence. "Ladeez and gen'l'men, thank you for coming to my 'umble establishment this evening." His words were met with a roar from the crowd. "Now, I know you didn't come 'ere to listen to me bellyache, now did ya. Nah, you came 'ere for a bit of somefink tasty, like. Am I right?" He cupped a hand to his ear. "I said, am I right?"

More cheers echoed round the room.

"I fought so. Now, 'ave we got a show for you tonight. This mass of mutt 'ere, he goes by the name of 'Itler and it's not cos he's only got one bollock." Beako chuckled at his own joke. "Comes in at sixty pounds, he does. Pure bred Staffy and mean as you like. Ten fights to date and all to the death. Obviously not 'is. And on the uvah side of the ring we 'ave our champion Rotty, Satan. So called because he's a mean fucking bastard. Black as night and reminds me of me dad. He was a vicious cunt too." The crowd roared at this.

Beako looked at the dogs in the centre of the ring straining at the metal chains looped around their necks. Each was restrained by Beako's handlers, blokes who wouldn't look out of place in a wrestling ring, all muscle and no neck. Both dogs belonged to Beako. Whatever happened on the evening, he would always come out quids up. So he was a dog down come the end of the evening. That didn't matter. There were always more mutts ready to be thrown into the ring whenever was needed.

"Let battle commence!"

The sound of metal chains being slipped was lost among the raucous baying of the surrounding mob. The handlers had sprung out of the ring at the same time as the two dogs lunged forward at each other. This was to be the fight of the year. Hitler versus Satan. Champion versus champion with one outright winner. And the money weighing down Beako's jacket was testament to the fervour whipped up for this evening.

The shouts became more aggressive as the fight progressed.

"Gerrup, you miserable mutt!"

"Rip his fuckin' froat out, you worthless piece of shit!"

"Kill the fuckin' cunt!"

Teeth tore into flesh, no ground was given by either dog. Saliva flew and mingled with blood making the floorboards slick. It was ten minutes before it was all over. Ten brutal, unforgiving minutes overlaid with a soundtrack of the worst of humanity.

At the end, Hitler limped out of the ring, tethered by his handler, whilst Satan lay unmoving.

Beako's pudgy fingers punched in the requisite numbers

on the pad inside his front door to deactivate the alarm. It had been a good night, a very good night, and now he wanted to relax for what was left of the evening.

First things first though.

He kept his jacket on as he shuffled through the opulence of his house. Life had been good to Beako ever since he started getting involved in the fights. Years had passed since then. Initially, Beako's operation had been a run of the mill bookies, taking scraps here and there on the horses, paying money on the outcome of the football: English, European and South American, it was all the same to him. But then the big companies had introduced all this online and mobile shite, with in game betting and loads of little side bets with odds he could never dream of matching designed to entice the punter. His revenues started to drop and he thought his days in the game would be numbered. Or at least until he stumbled upon the illicit world of dog fights. This was something your hardened gambler couldn't find on the high street. Here was something to set the juices running, to get the adrenaline pumping. The money was easy, and even easier for a man with Beako's balanced lack of morals and integrity. It didn't take long for him to move from simply running the book to owning the dogs. After less than a year in the game, Beako had his own kennels at his house with dogs stolen to order. He personally oversaw their upkeep and training. He knew his way round a whip and Taser, devices he used with a little too much enthusiasm.

Rediscovering the Ritzy had been a stroke of luck. His parents had taken him there when he was a kid towards the end of its heyday. His mum had had hopes that a little culture would rub off on him and let him escape the life they had become trapped in. His dad's fists had beaten any sense of culture out of him but it had taught him how to be a double hard bastard. After all, it's not the size of the dog but the size of the fight within it. Forty years later and he'd stumbled across the Ritzy whilst going round his old haunts in a fleeting trip of nostalgia. It was one of those properties which no one wanted to restore but no one could tear down for flats because of its 'historic significance' or some other such bullshit. Beako didn't care – it was the perfect venue for what he wanted. A large building in a rundown bit of town which the police had given up on. The type of area where the smackheads shot up openly on the streets and pissed blood in the gutters. Within a couple of years Beako 'owned' the town. He found he was generating a couple of grand a fight, and that was after paying out on winnings. And right now, tonight's winnings were foremost in his mind.

He passed through his hallway, into the reception area (his old man wouldn't believe he had a reception area) and turned right. Through the door was his study; his inner sanctum. He knelt, as if in prayer. Except he hadn't entered a church for the best part of twenty years, not since he had buried his folks, killed in an accidental fire. Rumours abounded at the time, whispered comments about the source of the fire, knowing nods exchanged about the timing being fortunate just when young Beako was strapped for cash. Those rumours died down quickly. Anyone repeating them was found with their tongue poking out from the opened skin of their neck.

Beako's fingers lifted the edge of the patterned rug covering the bulk of the floor space, easing it up before rolling it back. Underneath sat his safe, cemented into the floor and covered with a concealing wooden panel which matched the floorboards. He poked at a knot in the wood, a hidden button to release the panel, sending it sliding silently backwards out of sight. The safe was the best money could buy, or so the vendor had told him. Its face was formed of tungsten with an electronic keypad situated squarely in the centre. Beako punched in the code from memory, listening as the inner locks released themselves and clicked open. The safe's interior was compact, the size of two shoes boxes stacked on top of each other. It was fireproof, which made Beako feel more secure about the amount of cash he kept in there, along with emergency passports should the need arise. There was currently about fifty thousand pounds in notes sitting there, to which he added the best part of five grand he had taken over the evening. He'd process his earnings through the relevant channels over the coming weeks, make sure it was all nicely cleaned and paid into a reputable dummy account he used for such purposes.

The next hour was spent watching trash on his widescreen television. It had taken two men to install it, their backs and mouths complaining in unison at the weight of the thing. In the old days, the national anthem would have signalled the end to the evening's viewing. Nowadays it was the onset of the first infomercial – 'How to get your body toned ready for the beach.' Beako flicked the television off, not bothered enough to surf the myriad of channels at his fingertips, and trudged his way to bed. It was gone three in the morning.

He slumped onto the queen size mattress, shrugging his clothes off until he was down to his boxer shorts and vest. The contours of his gut were less flattering even than they had been when fully clothed. A double fold of stomach presented underneath the white fabric of his vest, a little flesh showing where the hem didn't quite meet with the top of his boxers. He had removed the gun he kept strapped to his ankle for protection and slipped it into the drawer of his bedside table. His grounds were alarmed and there was a guard at the gate to his estate but you never could be too careful.

Three minutes passed between Beako's head hitting the pillow and his falling asleep.

Agitated barking woke Beako. He chose to ignore it, rolling over and placing his head under the pillow. It would be the dogs at the back of the house. When he purchased the property, he had converted an old stable block towards the rear into kennels. Conditions were tight. Twenty cages fitted into a space which would not normally be contemplated for ten. It didn't matter to Beako. Life expectancy was measured in weeks for his inmates. So as long as they fed, drank and slept he was happy. Once a week he had someone come and clean the kennels out, using a jetwash to flush the floor of faeces, channelling them into a porcelain gunnel running down the edges of the interior. Like his safe, the cage locks were all electronically programmed, allowing him to release as many or few doors as he wanted. On days when he was feeling spiteful he would release all the cages when the cleaner was in there for no other reason than it amused him.

The cacophony outside was still in full chorus five minutes later.

"Drummond," snapped Beako into the intercom, the device embedded in the wall beside his bed connected to the main gate of his estate.

"Drummond, answer when I fucking well speak to you."

But there was no answer. Only a ghostly static chittering in the darkness.

"Fuck's sake," Beako muttered to himself. "I'll deal with it my bloody self then, shall I?"

He threw on a dressing gown, tightening the cloth belt around the bulge of his midriff. He opened his bedside drawer and slipped the pistol into the deep pockets of the gown. Tramping downstairs, he pulled on a pair of boots, the green rubber far from a perfect match with his current attire. Grabbing a torch from the back of a kitchen drawer he strode out into the night.

"Great!" he mumbled, a fine drizzle permeating the air, the sort which seeped its way into every part of your clothing. He could already feel droplets of water collecting on the tip of his nose, giving him the appearance of a leaking faucet with its pervasive drip, drip, drip. Drummond was going to have some explaining to do when he caught up with him.

Gravel shifted beneath his feet, the crunch an undertone to the baying dogs across the courtyard. Beako's left hand went to the gun nestled in his pocket, his other holding the torch in front of him. Beako wasn't a nervous man but there was something reassuring about the cold steel clamped against his palm. It balanced his general sense of unease, a forgotten instinct dragged from ancestors long dead who hunted with stick and flame. It screeched at him to drop the torch and run back to the safety of the house. It asked him why the security lights hadn't kicked in when he walked past the sensors or why Drummond was nowhere to be seen. It asked much and he ignored each interrogation from his psyche, bloody-minded stubbornness forcing him forward. Beako backed down for no one and he wasn't going to turn nancy boy and run screaming from the dark.

"Come out, you fucker!" Aggressive words shouted into a world of shadows.

No one answered. He hadn't thought they would. A psychiatrist would have told Beako he was channelling his fear, preparing for fight or flight, but a head doctor's couch was the last place he would ever position himself.

Gravel gave way to packed earth underfoot, marking the perimeter of the converted stable block. Here the baying was at its loudest. There was a full contingent in the kennels bar one; Satan. His body would be in the early stages of rigor mortis at the bottom of Mortlake Canal, stuffed unceremoniously into a torn hessian sack weighted with rocks. Beako had lost count of the bodies rotting under the water while day trippers sailed past overhead.

Beako perched on his toes, peering through the window set into the main door. Torchlight swung from left to right, hunting the shadows for any sign of an intruder but there was nothing. The light seemed to agitate the dogs further, whipping them up into more of a frenzy, if that were even possible. Dogs were yapping at the metal bars at the front of their cages, rubbing their sides raw on the tight, encompassing mesh which squeezed in on them from either side. Others were scratching at the concrete floor, attempting to dig their way out beneath the entrance to their prisons.

"Stupid fucking mutts." And then something happened which made Beako freeze. The dogs stopped barking. Each and every one of them dropped to the floor, paws crossed over their muzzles. A new sound replaced the ferocity. This one was timid. It said *'don't hurt me, whatever you do, don't hurt me.'* A high pitched whimpering which Beako associated with his sessions with the Tazer. His mind told him they had heard his voice. It said they were scared of him, knowing who their lord and master was. This was the same part of his mind which had fought the urge to run previously. And this time it lost.

Beako's feet were carrying him back to the house before he realised what he was doing. His stride was ungainly, it was something he was unaccustomed to, especially in rubber boots with the tail of his gown flapping behind him, his gait that of a sloth learning how to run. In one hand he held the flashlight, in the other his gun, the pistol leaping to his grip from instinct. The light from his torch bounced off surfaces, revealing bits of brickwork on outbuildings, bits of gravel on the path ahead, the normally orange chipped stone showing white in the beam. Blackness moved in the shadows, darkness on night. There was something out there with him. He couldn't see it, not well enough to make out more than an impression but he knew it could see him. There was menace there. A malevolence which meant him harm. And it was toying with him. It had lured him out here He was shouting as he ran, screaming for Drummond, wanting to know *where the fuck* he was, desperate pleas which he knew wouldn't be answered. Then he was at the back door to his house, the rear face of the brick building dwarfing him. Waiting for him on the steps leading to his kitchen was Drummond.

Drummond's body was limp, positioned in such a way which suggested he had suffered. Arms and legs were contorted out of shape, twisted as if fighting off an assailant who kept attacking and attacking and attacking. Each foray had come at speed, darting in from impossible angles which forced Drummond to turn and writhe to fend off each assault. Beako played the torchlight along Drummond's corpse. His mind put together pieces of a puzzle he had no desire to solve. The open gash in Drummond's neck, his throat torn open and the windpipe wrenched out into the night air. The lack of any other cuts or contusions on his body as if all the violence Drummond had been subjected to had been imaginary, some drug-fuelled fantasy he had been trying to stave off. And that might have been true if it weren't for the windpipe. The final piece of the puzzle rested in Drummond's right hand. The flesh beneath his fingernails was still wet, glistening in the torchlight. The skin was Drummond's, a pale white which came from his Celtic ancestry. Everything came together to form one single unasked for question: what would force a man to rip out his own throat?

Beako lifted his head to look to the house. He saw movement. His gun was raised, a single shot rung off before he realised he was shooting at his own reflection in the darkened surface of the window. The shot had been wild, the bullet burying itself deep into the mortar several feet to the left of the glass. It left Beako staring at a fat old man dressed in a white embroidered dressing gown, his thinning hair matted over a pale crown by drizzle which had turned to rain. The farcical sight of a man used to being in control who now stood helpless over the corpse of a man whose first name he didn't even know. Except that wasn't Beako. He wasn't going to go into the night quietly. He wasn't going to go the way of Drummond. Beako was a fighter and tonight he was going to live.

Movement flickered in the window behind Beako's reflection.

Beako spun and shot, crouching like he had forced

characters to do in the military games he played online. It didn't matter that they moved more fluidly than he did. This was real life. He wanted to be low in case Drummond's killer was armed, to make a smaller target of himself even as he loosed off two bullets. That was what mattered. Any advantage to staying alive. It took a moment for his eyes to pick out the dead form of Drummond's killer.

The torch had fallen to the ground as Beako turned, using both hands to steady his shot. It lay at an angle which picked out the bulk of the courtyard, sending light across the gravel and trailing off before it reached the kennels in the distance. A hunched shape was caught in the fullness of the beam, its torso positioned where Beako had aimed. His shots had been true, targeting a couple of feet above the ground where the attacker had been crawling. The bullets had found their mark but they hadn't made a difference. After all, how do you kill something which had already died once that evening?

Satan's upper lip curled in warning. Ghostly paws padded over the gravel, stepping over each other to circle round to Beako's left, but they made no sound. All Beako could hear was the incessant whimpering rising from the kennels. Except the mood was changing. The whimpers becoming bolder, turning to full-throated barks as the dogs sensed blood in the air.

Beako picked up the torch, turning his body with each step Satan took, his eyes focused on this thing, this creature; he wouldn't say ghost, they didn't exist. All the while trying to comprehend what he was seeing.

"You're dead." The words were quiet. "You're dead. I saw you die."

Satan growled.

"I saw you die!"

Satan stopped moving. Drummond was behind him now and Beako was once again facing the house. Both circled round in a slow dance of death. The torchlight fell fully on Satan's form, the beam wavering in Beako's hand. Even as Satan crouched low, lips curled back, his body cast no shadow.

Three shots rang out followed by the click of an empty chamber and then another. Each bullet passed through Satan and thudded into the still warm corpse of Drummond. If he believed in God, Beako would have offered up a prayer of salvation, calling for forgiveness. But there was no God to listen here either way. Only a devil dog with a grudge.

Beako turned and ran.

Rainwater splashed where puddles were forming on the ground, droplets caught in the wild beam of the torch. He had no idea if Satan was following, no tell-tale sound of paws running on loose stones to indicate how long he had before the beast pounced. Curiosity is a powerful motivator. It makes us do things we shouldn't. Beako was no different.

Three quarters of the way to the stable blocks, his toe caught the ground as he turned his head to look behind him. Beako's body hit the floor, his face scraping against the rough surface, tearing open a strip of red across his cheek. The torch went flying from his hand and skittered across the courtyard, batteries spilling from its stem. Everything descended into darkness.

Behind him, Beako heard a growl.

Beako scurried forwards, stumbling on all fours, blindly feeling his way in the darkness. He expected to feel teeth sink into his ankle or a weighted paw to come down on his back. But nothing came. With each metre he covered a sense of hope dawned on him. He thought of Drummond's corpse, the lack of teeth or claw marks. It couldn't hurt him. Phantom teeth with no bite. It could trick him, force him to rip his own throat out like Drummond. But he wouldn't. He was too smart for that. Even as gravel turned to earth and he leaned his body against the side of the kennels he grabbed that one thought, singing it in his mind above the chorus of dogs behind him. He could feel cold, unnatural breath on his face and hear the low growl of a beast in his ear but no tearing teeth. And with each second the words played over and over, growing stronger and stronger as he knew they were true.

"It's a ghost, it can't hurt you," he muttered, fear making a believer out of him, "it's a ghost, it can't hurt you, it's a ghost, it can't hurt you."

He kept recanting the same words over and over again to himself, forcing his mind to forget the image of Drummond who had torn out his own throat, a man twice his size. He kept repeating his mantra, word after word, his own holy prayer of protection, only stopping when he felt the breath lift from around his face and throat, when he heard the sound of barking stopping behind him. A pause in the cacophony punctuated by a clank of metal and then silence. Beako's throat constricted, he fought to swallow, finding God as realisation dawned and hoping he would save an old sinner like him. But God said nothing. All Beako heard was the sound of paws on concrete, the low level growl of a pack of canines eager for retribution accompanied by the creak of a large stable door being pushed back.

 MICHAEL BRAY is a bestselling author / screenwriter. Influenced from an early age by the suspense horror of authors such as Stephen King, Richard Laymon, Shaun Hutson, James Herbert & Brian Lumley, along with TV shows like Tales from the Crypt & The Twilight Zone, his work touches on the psychological side of horror, teasing the reader's nerves and willing them to keep turning the pages. Several of his titles are currently being translated into multiple languages and he recently sold movie rights to his novel, *Meat*, with production planned to take place in the near future. A screenplay written by Bray and Matt Shaw, based on their co-written novel *Monster*, was picked up for distribution by Mandala Films, with both Bray and Shaw producing and directing the movie, taking his career into new territory as he looks to write more for both the literary world and the screen. When not writing he loves to read, watch TV and follows his beloved football team, Leeds United. His website is at **michaelbrayauthor.com**

 STEVEN CHAPMAN is a horror author, who has been abusing the English language since 1984. He enjoys nothing more than a good blood-curdling tale, and spends far too much of his time reading, watching, and writing horror. His work has featured in anthologies alongside Ramsey Campbell and Josh Malerman, and he still panics at the thought of

having to sign a book. He blogs about writing, sometimes coherently, at **stevenchapmanwriter.com**

✳ ✳ ✳

 LILY CHILDS has an obsession with misunderstood demons and takes unsavoury delight in Victorian underworlds, twisted myths and the necrotic. "Queen Bitch", written the year before the divine songsmith David Bowie's untimely death, takes its name from the track on his 1971 album, *Hunky Dory*. The Queen Bitch in Lily's story is based on a very real, extremely vicious terrier named Sophie who the author had the misfortune to encounter in the 1980s. A writer of dark horror, crime and ghost stories, Lily has just completed her first novel, a supernatural asylum chiller. Recently published short stories include "Woe, Violent Water" in *Tales from the Lake Vol. 3* (Crystal Lake Publishing), "The Vile Glib of Gideon Wicke" *The Black Room Manuscripts Vol, 2* (The Sinister Horror Company) and *In Search of Silver Boughs* (KnightWatch Press). Read a selection of Lily's horror and crime stories in *Cabaret of Dread; Volume 1*. Follow her on Facebook at **lilychildsfeardom**, Twitter **@LilyChilds** and at **lilychildsfeardom.blogspot.co.uk**. Lily lives by the sea in the south of England. She has no dog in which to trust, but does share her house with a golden-eyed black cat, Scarlet.

✳ ✳ ✳

 RAY CLULEY is a British Fantasy Award winner with stories published in various magazines and anthologies. Some of these have been republished in 'best of' volumes, including Ellen Datlow's *Best Horror of the Year* series and *Nightmares: A New Decade of Modern Horror*, as well as Steve Berman's *Wilde Stories: The Year's Best Gay Speculative Fiction*, and Benoît Domis's *Ténèbres*. He has been translated into French, Polish, and Hungarian, with Chinese coming soon and a German translation of his novella *Water For Drowning* rumoured to be in the works. New stories will be appearing soon – or have recently appeared – in *Black Static* and a sea themed anthology, *Devil and the Deep*. His first collection, *Probably Monsters*, is available from ChiZine Publications. He is currently putting together a second while working on a novel.

 GARY FRY lives in Dracula's Whitby, literally around the corner from where Bram Stoker was staying when he was thinking about that character. Gary has a PhD in psychology, but his first love is literature. He is the author of many short story collections, novellas and novels. He was the first author in PS Publishing's Showcase series, and none other than Ramsey Campbell has described him as "a master." Gary warmly welcomes all to his web presence at **www.gary-fry.com**

⁂

D.T. GRIFFITH is fascinated by all things dark, gritty, and dystopian, and hangs out in the periphery of the horror and dark fiction genres. He has worked as a professional designer, illustrator, and writer since the 1990s in the marketing, branding, communication, and ecommerce fields. He draws inspiration from classic and modern works alike, spanning a full range of literary masters, surrealist painters, comedians, and punk rock musicians. D.T. Griffith holds an MFA in Creative and Professional Writing and a BFA in Visual Art. He lives in his home state of Connecticut, USA. You can find him on Twitter **@dtgriffith** and find more of his work through **dtgriffith.com**

AMELIA MANGAN was born in London in 1983, and currently lives in Sydney, Australia. Her debut novel, *Release*, was published in 2015 by Nightscape Press, and her short stories have been featured in many anthologies, including one – "The Edifice of Dust", published in *The Hyde Hotel* anthology, 2016 – that received an Honorable Mention in Ellen Datlow's *The Best Horror of the Year, Vol. 9.* Her story "Blue Highway" won Yen Magazine's first annual short story competition in 2013; The Book Smugglers selected her story "The

Bridegroom" as their website's first annual featured Halloween tale in 2015. She can be found on Twitter **@AmeliaMangan** and Facebook **facebook.com/amelia.mangan**.
(Photo credit – Kris Baum)

WILLIAM MEIKLE is a Scottish writer, now living in Canada, with over twenty novels published in the genre press and more than 300 short story credits in thirteen countries. He has books available from a variety of publishers including Dark Regions Press, DarkFuse and Dark Renaissance, and his work has appeared in a large number of professional anthologies and magazines. He lives in Newfoundland with whales, bald eagles and icebergs for company. When he's not writing he drinks beer, plays guitar, and dreams of fortune and glory. Find him at **williammeikle.com**

ADAM MILLARD is the author of twenty-two novels, twelve novellas, and more than two hundred short stories, which can be found in various collections, magazines, and anthologies. Probably best known for his post-apocalyptic and comedy-horror fiction, Adam also writes fantasy/horror for children, as well as bizarro fiction for

several publishers. His work has recently been translated for the German market. **www.adammillard.co.uk**

PHIL SLOMAN is a writer of dark fiction. His novella *Becoming David* was shortlisted for a British Fantasy Society Best Newcomer award in 2017. Phil likes to peek behind the curtain of reality and see what might be lurking there. Sometimes he writes down what he sees. His short stories can be found throughout various anthologies. In the humdrum of everyday life, Phil lives with an understanding wife and a trio of vagrant cats who tolerate their human slaves. There are no bodies buried beneath the patio as far as he is aware. Occasionally Phil can be found wasting time on Facebook or at **insearchofperdition.blogspot.co.uk** – come say hi.

MARK WEST was born in Northamptonshire in 1969 and now lives there with his wife Alison and their young son Matthew. Since discovering the small press in 1998 he has published over eighty short stories, two novels (*In The Rain With The Dead* and *Conjure*), a novelette (*The Mill*), a chapbook (*What Gets Left Behind*), two collections (*Strange Tales* and *Things We Leave Behind*) and three novellas (*Drive*, which was nominated for a British

Fantasy Award, *The Lost Film* and *The Factory*). He has more short stories and novellas forthcoming and he is currently working on a novel. Away from writing, he enjoys reading, walking, cycling, watching films and playing Dudeball with his son. He can be contacted through his website at **markwest.org.uk** and is also on Twitter **@MarkEWest**